HIS WOMAN OF SUBSTANCE

CAROLYN FAULKNER

Published by Blushing Books
An Imprint of
ABCD Graphics and Design, Inc.
A Virginia Corporation
977 Seminole Trail #233
Charlottesville, VA 22901

His Woman of Substance
Carolyn Faulkner

EBook ISBN: 978-1-63954-498-1
Print ISBN: 978-1-63954-499-8

Cover Art by ABCD Graphics & Design
This book contains fantasy themes appropriate for mature readers only.
Nothing in this book should be interpreted as Blushing Books' or
the author's advocating any non-consensual sexual activity.

Chapter 1

FUCK.

Fuck, fuck, fuck, fuck.

Fuckity-fuck-fuck-fuck.

Jane was sitting in her usual spot in the back of the bar, not too far from the bathrooms, and discovering belatedly that she'd let her friends go without realizing that she'd consumed entirely too much alcohol. She'd gotten up, intending to head for said bathrooms, and then had to sit down just as quickly, so that she didn't end up in an undignified heap on the floor.

She caught the waitress' eye, which was much easier to do now that the crowd had thinned out. She thought she was practically the only person in the bar, although she didn't look up from her phone to confirm that thought.

"Christie, can I have a large glass of water and a cup of coffee?"

Christie chuckled. "Feeling it?"

She frowned. "Yes, unfortunately."

"I'm surprised. You can usually pack it away. But that tequila will sneak up on you sometimes."

"Yeah, and on a relatively empty stomach. Thanks so much, dieting—not!" She'd totally forgotten to account for her new eating habits and how they might affect her alcohol tolerance.

Christie laughed. "I hear ya! Just another of the many evils of dieting! I'll have that right over to you."

"You're a doll. Thank you."

She pulled up Uber for ride. There was no way she was going to drive her little car home when she felt like this. She'd just Uber back tomorrow morning to collect it when she woke up—hopefully not feeling as if someone had dragged her tongue along the carpet, if she was able to convince herself to drink enough water before she crawled into bed.

But as she was looking down at her phone, a shadow fell over her. A very big shadow.

And if she used her peripheral vision, she could see that the man casting it was wearing a pair of very old, disreputable boots, probably about a size thirteen or so.

She knew immediately who it was standing over her, not really crowding her, but then, even being in the same universe as he was, was always going to make her feel crowded.

She was uncomfortably aware of the fact that he also still managed to make her feel small, and that was no easy feat since she definitely wasn't a small woman.

Jane staunchly refused to acknowledge him, childish thought it may be, even though she well knew that he wasn't the most patient of men—about some things, anyway. She certainly could remember times when he was extremely patient with her, but she did her best to eradicate those thoughts, to wipe them from her mind one by one as they appeared in her head.

And kept appearing, growing more and more obscene

each time, until she had to worry about leaving a stain on her skirt that he was sure to notice at some point and take it the wrong way.

He certainly wasn't a fan of defiance of any kind, either, but then she hardy thought this qualified.

She had to acknowledge baldly to herself, though, that it didn't really matter whether *she* thought it was. It mattered whether or not *he* thought it was!

Or it used to, anyway.

Of course, that was extremely hard to do when he was standing there looking down at her, mountain that he was, and it was growing worse by the second. She could smell him —in an entirely too delicious way for her inebriated nerves to handle. He was wearing the same distinctive, musky, masculine cologne he always had, and that achingly familiar scent was complimented by two others that set her traitorous heart and southern parts to aching in a terrifyingly familiar way. The first was the leather from the jacket he always wore— that was just as bedraggled as his boots, or more so.

And the second was simply *him*.

He smelled like home to her. Always had. Probably always would.

That was another thought that played hell with her, that highlighted the fact that she hadn't gotten over him nearly as much as she would have liked to think she had. Jane's eyes filled for a second, but she ruthlessly fought the tears back. There was no way in hell she was going to cry in front of him.

She'd already shed too many tears on account of Elijah Jackson Ridgeway. She was determined there would be no more.

"Jane."

The man had a voice that would have made him millions if he'd just be willing to read porn out loud on the Internet somewhere, no doubt. Hell, it didn't even have to be porn, she was ashamed to admit. He could read the instructions for how to put together an Ikea coffee table and she'd get just as wet every time as she wished she wasn't getting right now.

Without looking up at him, she answered in as neutral a tone as she could summon, "Eli."

He didn't respond immediately, which was unusual for him. But apparently thinking about what he was going to say hadn't made any difference in how autocratic it sounded.

"I'm going to take you home."

It wasn't a question; it was a statement. And that was very Eli. He wasn't about to risk the idea of her saying, "No," so he assumed her assent and intended to just move on from there to proceed in the fashion he most preferred.

But her mind reminded her that it was also very like Eli to try to take care of someone, especially a woman.

Especially her.

Jane snorted softly, still not looking away from her phone, even though she wasn't seeing what she was looking at. Every scintilla of her attention was on him, as was usual for her.

Old habits died very hard, apparently.

"Not fucking likely."

He continued to stand there next to her, and she knew exactly what he wanted to do. Out of the corner of her eye, she could see his fingers flexing restlessly, as if in anticipation of action. He wanted to pick her up bodily—which he was more than capable of doing. He'd done it when she weighed more than she did now, over her vociferous complaints, and as if she was a size zero.

It was in her mind to warn him not to do it, but she stifled the impulse. She was going to speak to him as little as possible, drink her water and her coffee, and wait for her ride to arrive. She was determined she wasn't even going to give him the satisfaction of asking him to go away.

More softly said than his last edict, but still dominant and commanding as fuck, he intoned, "You're drunk, and I'll make sure you get home safely, if I have to pick you up and carry you out, myself."

That only served to point out to her how well she still knew him.

She gave him a one word response that still let him know that she considered it none of his business. "Uber." Then she continued playing Words with Friends on her phone. Not that she'd managed to put her letters together into any kind of coherent word with him standing there like that, as if he had every right to do so. She couldn't concentrate on the game, could barely see it, and had no idea with whom she was playing at this point. But that didn't matter. All that mattered was that she stay calm and carry on.

He scoffed. "You'd rather pay to get into a car with a stranger—when you're already falling down drunk—than ride home for free with me?"

Jane ignored him, wearing a big smirk that suggested that an idiot would have known that.

His tone was firmly back in dictatorial mode—emphasis on the "dic". He wasn't used to being disobeyed or ignored, especially not by her. "Cancel it, Jane."

Dear God, her name from his lips conjured up even memories of how he'd whispered it hotly into her ear, breathed it prayerfully against her most intimate places, and screamed it out in the throes of ecstasy she had brought him to.

Again, she ignored him, knowing full well that she did so at her own peril.

He waited—less than patiently—for her to say something, anything, then he crouched down next to her chair with surprising grace for such a big man. And they weren't even eye level then, either, she grimaced.

His words were very soft and very firm. "I'm going to take you home, so I can make sure that you've gotten there safely. I suggest that you cancel the Uber, or you're going to have wasted the driver's time."

That, at least, got her to stop playing, he was glad to see, although she'd stubbornly yet to actually look at him.

He'd been surprised to see her in a bar—she'd never had alcohol around him, but he guessed she'd changed some habits. Not that he could blame her. She looked thinner, too, by quite a bit, but he wasn't going to say that to her. His mama hadn't raised no fools.

He wanted nothing more than to do as he'd threatened and sweep her up into his arms and carry her out of there— not because he thought she couldn't handle her own life. Not because he saw her as helpless and weak; he knew she was a very smart, very capable woman. But that didn't stop very primitive urges from coursing through him, and they were all screaming that he needed to protect her—from drinking too much at a bar, from other men who might also come to want her so badly that no amount of masturbating soothed the ache, and, most devastatingly, from himself.

That was not taking into consideration that he ached to have her in his arms again, and if that was the only way to achieve that…

She sighed softly under her breath, but he, of course, heard it. He knew he was the last person she wanted to ever see again, and that he was on her last nerve, and that she was likely fighting back tears. All of which only made him just that much more determined to make sure she got home safely.

"I assume that telling you to go away would be just a

waste of my breath." That, too, was a statement rather than a question, issued in a tone that was so unlike her usual very pleasant one so as to cause the ever-present ache in his chest to become much worse.

Still, Eli couldn't help but want to grin at that, but he did his level best to suppress it.

"You assume correctly, little girl."

Christ, he was killing her—as if he hadn't done that—or awfully close to it—once already. And once was more than enough for her.

When she finally did look at him, it was to roll her eyes exaggeratedly and snort softly, and he knew it wasn't at his confirmation of her assumption. It was at the endearment he'd very deliberately used.

It surprised him when she pushed her chair back all of a sudden and skirted deftly around him. He'd immediately stood up, ready to steady her if she was as uneasy on her feet as she had been a while ago. But she was feeling at least somewhat better now, it seemed, leaving him to trail after her like a lost lamb.

"Here you go, Christie." She handed the woman a couple of twenties for the evening's libations, along with a liberal tip. "Are you off now?"

"No, hon, I'm closing." The other woman eyed Eli and shrugged. "Sorry."

"What about Pickle?"

"Pickle's not on tonight, and Henny's gone already."

"Batting a thousand, as usual," she grumbled under her breath. Then she smiled up at Christie. "Thanks, anyway. Have a good night!"

"You, too." Still giving Eli the stink eye, she asked, "Want me to walk you to your Uber?"

"She's cancelling her Uber. I'm going to drive her home," Eli informed her, in no uncertain terms.

"That's why I offered," the woman replied without backing down in the least, which made Jane chuckle.

Eli scowled, which was a look that threw terror into most people's hearts.

But neither of the women around him seemed in the least fazed by it. Come to think of it, neither was his sister anymore. He must be losing his touch.

Jane was waffling, but then she heard the notification that her Uber was going to arrive soon, and she just headed for the door.

Eli easily got there before her short legs could carry her and held the door open. Her "thank you" was barely mumbled and barely civil, but automatic nonetheless.

Unfortunately, those same short legs prevented her from getting to the car, too, before Eli did. It wasn't as if she could run anywhere without knocking herself out with the girls. Seconds later, despite the fact that she had tried to yell and catch his attention so he wouldn't leave, she watched as he departed. Eli put his wallet back in his back pocket as he straightened and turned to catch her eye, looking much too smug for Jane to stand.

So, she just changed course and began to head for the parking lot. She rummaged around in her pocketbook for her keys, found them, and as she was rearranging things and not paying attention to him, she found them scooped out of her hand and into his big one.

Jane put her hand out to him, in mute demand, her mouth a grim, angry line.

He seemed to soften—a bit—and she remembered that coaxing tone well. "Jane, less than ten minutes ago, I watched you stand up and nearly fall down again, you were so drunk. Can you really tell me that you're fine to drive now? I'd sooner let you take the Uber than drive yourself home."

God, she hated him with every part of her body and parts of other people's, too!

Without a word, she stalked over in the relative darkness to his jalopy and stood by the door, waiting for him to unlock it.

"That's someone else's, honey. My car's a bit newer than that." He held out a fob and there was a beep from a car across the lot—something big and muscular and barely leashed, like himself.

Well, at least in his case, she knew for a fact that he wasn't compensating for a small dick.

It hurt to hear it every time he did it, but she ignored the endearment in favor of trudging over to the other car. She pulled on the passenger's door handle, but couldn't get in. The son of a bitch hadn't unlocked the passenger's side, just so he could walk over to her and do so, opening the door for her as he always had.

When Jane was seated, he even presumed to lean in and try to latch her seatbelt for her.

"If you touch that thing, you're going to withdraw a bloody stump," she threatened through her teeth, pulling it across her body and fastening it herself.

Well, it was more than she'd said to him all evening. There was that, at least, he supposed. Threatening bodily harm wasn't exactly what he'd been going for, but he'd take whatever he could get at this point. He knew he didn't really deserve anything better than that, although he had hopes of making her feel much less homicidal towards him in the near future.

Well, maybe not the near future.

Now that they were underway, he put her keys down on the console between them, saying in that low, sexy voice of his, "Thank you for letting me take you home, Jane."

She snatched them away as if she thought he was going

to try to catch her hand and hold it if she didn't, making him grimace at the reminder that he couldn't do that anymore.

She still wasn't looking at him and was acting as if she'd rather be in the car with pretty much anyone but him. Darth Vader, Hitler, and Jeffrey Dahmer all came to mind as replacements she'd probably prefer over his company. And he had only himself to blame for that.

He knew it was a weak start, but he wanted to get her talking. They'd always communicated so well. He'd missed that terribly. In the days and weeks afterward, he'd tried to call her and text her and email her. For the first day or so, they were simply ignored. After that, they all went exactly nowhere—returned undeliverable. She'd been ruthlessly efficient at shutting him out of her life. And, the bald-faced truth was that he couldn't blame her in the least.

His lame conversational gambit sent her digging in her pocketbook again. This time, she came up with earbuds, which she proceeded to plug in and use. He couldn't tell what she was listening to or what she was doing without running them off the road.

So, he reached over and pulled the closest of them out.

"I said, thank you for letting me take you home."

She put the bud back in.

He pulled it out.

Eli raised his voice ridiculously high, which made it crack badly, as if he was imitating her. "No, Eli, thank *you* for taking me home!"

If she didn't hate him for all she was worth, she might have laughed at that. The bud went back in her ear, but it was tugged out a second later.

"Do you like the car?"

She would have tried to crane herself as far away from him as she could in hopes of getting out of his reach, but that was a pipe dream. In these bucket seats—as nice as they were—her ass was going nowhere, to say nothing of the fact that the man had an unnaturally long reach to go along with his freakishly long legs. Finally, she just left the bud out and continued to not listen to—or watch—an episode of *Castle Rock* on Hulu.

He was too damned distracting for her to comprehend it, not that she was going to let him know that.

In a last-ditch effort to get her attention, he tugged on the iPhone itself, and as a result, the car swerved a bit to the right.

"Fucking hell! And you thought I wouldn't be safe with an Uber driver?" Jane yelled.

"Language, Jane," he scolded softly, and she felt her cheeks flush painfully hot. "You don't think I'll pull this car over right here, right now, and put you over my knee?"

She was outraged at what he was saying but not sure how to best express it, so she said nothing, blinking back tears of frustration.

And, no, she wouldn't put that past him in the least.

"You're perfectly fine with me. She's very responsive," he purred. "Just like—"

"If you finish that sentence, I'm going to punch you in the fucking nuts, and I don't give a fuck whether doing so kills us both."

His equipment immediately tried to crawl back inside him at her words—and the unnaturally calm, if emotion filled, tone in which they were delivered. She was royally pissed, but he also heard the tears she was suppressing in her voice, as much as she tried to cover them up.

Eli shifted uneasily in his seat, and his, "I'm sorry," was undeniably heartfelt. "About everything. I'm sorry."

Jane tried to go back to her phone, but it seemed her thoughts and feelings were in too much of an uproar for her to concentrate on it. They both knew some of it was the alcohol she'd consumed, but the rest of it was all his fault.

At least she wasn't playing on that damned phone any more. But now, he couldn't think of what to say to her to engage her in any kind of conversation—even an angry one, on her part.

And before he could think of anything, they were at her place, and she was out of the car practically before it came to a stop. He had intended to walk her to her door, even open it for her, if she would allow it. But that would not be happening any time soon.

He did, however, wait until he could see that she'd gotten into her house before he drove away. It was the least he could do—the very, very least.

"Three guesses who was in the bar last night, that I didn't find out about until he was standing next to me, demanding to take me home because I was drunk," she asked as she plopped down on the lounge chair next to the pool at her best friend's house the next night.

"Oh, I know—it was Eli."

Jane glared up at her friend. "You knew he was there?"

Sheila shrugged. "I thought you knew and were playing it cool. And day-um, those worn jeans clung to that beautiful ass of his—he looked scrumptious!"

Jane's expression grew dangerously dark, prompting her friend to say, "Sorry!" It had been more than several months since Jane's life had fallen apart, and she had been handling it almost unsettlingly well, so Sheila wasn't always sure how Jane was going to take things.

"I didn't know you were drunk," Sheila said quickly, hoping to distract her friend from the murderous thoughts she was apparently dwelling on. "You've had much more than that and been straight as an arrow."

"Yeah, but I'm eating a lot less than I used to, Sheil. I had all of that booze—which was a no-no, by the way—and all I had to eat yesterday was a carefully measured cup of oatmeal for breakfast with a carefully measured half cup of one percent, four carefully measured ounces of chicken with four equally carefully measured ounces of mixed veggies for lunch, along with two tablespoons of *I Can Definitely Believe This Shit Ain't Butter*, and I had nothing for dinner at all. You know what I would have eaten usually. All of those carby bagels and muffins and burgers with fries, and you damned well know I would have ordered something horrendous to eat while we were drinking—at least onion rings or nachos or whatever else. All that shit used to sop up all of the liquor I put away."

"Yeah, I hadn't thought about it, but I guess the skinnier you get, the cheaper a date you'll be!"

Jane frowned as if puzzled at whether she'd just been complimented or insulted. "Thanks?"

"So what happened?" Her friend leaned closer, eager to hear every juicy bit of gossip she could.

"What else? Eli is still Eli. You know what a force of nature that man is. The cheating, lying bastard says 'jump', and ninety-nine-point nine percent of the people around him say, 'yes, Sir, may I have another?'" She conveniently ignored the fact that he'd made her say just that on more than one occasion.

Sheila looked a bit confused. "I think you might have mixed your metaphors, or scrambled your memes, or something like that there."

"Well, you got the gist. He insisted he was going to take me home."

"So?"

Jane drew in a deep breath and exhaled her very reluctant answer. "He took me home."

Her friend practically jumped out of her chair with excitement at hearing this monumental news. "He did?"

"No one from the bar could do it—Christie was working late and the cooks were gone. I had an Uber ordered by the time the asshole came over to me, but he, of course, with his effing stilt legs got to him before me. He paid the guy off to go away, and when I got my keys out, the mofo grabbed them out of my hand, and he had the audacity to remind me that the reason he'd come over was because he'd seen me wobble a little when I got up to leave about ten minutes before."

Sheila immediate became a turncoat. "Then good for him, I say!"

"You had better take that back, missy!" She gave her best friend since kindergarten her most intimidating glare.

But Sheila didn't back down. "I will not. If Eli kept you from becoming a bloodstain on Route 45 last night, then more power to him," she stated defiantly. But Sheila wasn't a fool. She immediately followed it up with a much more conciliatory, "You know how horrible that road is, Jane. Lots of people lose control on it when they're sober. If the choice is between live, pissed at me you and dead, not pissed at me you, I choose the former, and I'm glad he kept you safe." Sheila peeped up at her friend, who didn't look as if she'd softened much. "The bastard!"

That got her. "Damn straight! Fuck him and his potentially lifesaving chivalrous tendencies! Who the fuck does he think he is, anyway?"

"*Yeah!*" Sheila agreed enthusiastically. Then she reconsidered, her face scrunched up as she puzzled. "Wait, what?"

"Just agree with me that he's a worthless piece of—"

"Six-foot-four if he's an inch, muscles bulging beneath a

shirt that can barely contain them, thick salt and pepper hair, beardy goodness—" She'd gotten lost there somewhere.

Jane actually leaned over and got in Sheila's face, growling, "Excuse me? Do I have a traitor in my midst?"

"Goddamned son of a bitch!" Sheila finished with gusto.

"That's much better!"

"But you have to admit that he's damned fine."

"No. I. Do. Not."

"Right." Then she muttered under her breath, "But he is."

Jane snarled at her, and that brought Sheila nicely to heel for the rest of their evening.

The fact that Jane agreed with her friend's description of her ex—even now—was of no matter whatsoever.

Across town, though, it was another story entirely, as Eli indulged a bit more than he usually did while sitting in his beat up old recliner in his lonely living room. Even his usually adoring dog was giving him accusatory looks. He had one hand looking at his phone—not looking for porn to watch, but, instead, scrolling through the texts and emails they'd shared while they were together, with his other hand wrapped around his iron spike of a dick.

Chapter 2

TWO YEARS EARLIER...

"You should be careful that you don't end up earning yourself a swat, too," came his deep rumble from behind her.

At first, Jane Medford barely dared to move. Dear God, was he talking to her? He couldn't have been talking to her— men that looked like Elijah Ridgeway didn't say things like that to women who looked like her. Hell, they didn't even so much as notice women like her! Why, when there was a gaggle of lithe sylphs whose eyes followed him much more blatantly than hers ever would. Their gazes were overt and covetous. Hers leaned much more towards wistful and ador- ing. Well, most of the time, anyway.

And, as her mother's shrill voice rang loudly through her head, saying what it had said to her throughout her entire childhood and adolescence—and she'd expected to hear it again on her deathbed, although she didn't—'men don't like fat girls'.

She'd been dragged to Weight Watchers when she was just eleven, to her horror and utter humiliation. Her mother had put her on every possible type of diet imaginable all her life. It got to the point that, as of about seventh grade, she refused to fund Jane's hot lunch account so that she'd be forced to skip at least one meal. And none of it had helped, of course. In fact, the situation had just gotten worse and worse. The more her mother berated her for being overweight, the more Jane binged and ate in secret.

She was a hundred and fifty pounds in the seventh grade, and she couldn't do a pull up. Mrs. Bove, the girls' physical education teacher, had given her a disgusted look that everyone had seen, of course, and that she assumed she'd be able to remember all of her days, along with all of the other slings and arrows she'd endured because of her size. Someone she didn't even know in their small town—who wasn't much older than she was—had walked by her on her way home from school one day and just flat out said, "You need to lose weight."

Jane felt as if, anytime she ate anything in public, everyone was watching her, as if to ask why she was eating when she was already so fat. Hell, when she'd first gone to buffets as an adult, several people had taken it upon themselves to tell her just that or to snicker and point and laugh. She wasn't sure which was worse. Someone had even written "hippo" on her yearbook page, but Sheila was one of the editors of it, thankfully, and was able to remove it before it went to print.

It had taken leaving for college for her to find herself a bit. It was much needed time away from her overbearing, hypercritical mother, who continually compared her physically to her best friend, Sheila, who had 'such a cute figure'. Those four years hadn't been a perfect time—there had been a pretty cruel growing pain here or there, one in particular that was down to one very nasty male student she'd thought liked her.

She wasn't quite as self-actualized as she intended to

become, but she was certainly feeling a lot better about herself than she used to. College had offered her more independence and more acceptance than she'd ever expected to find anywhere, and she had blossomed. Jane had graduated near the top of her class, getting her degree in elementary education, and was about to start her job as a fourth-grade teacher this fall in the school system in which she'd attended herself.

Maybe she should have found a job far away, but Jane'd come back to this place because it was home. Plus, she wanted to be near Sheila, who was still her best friend despite four years spent mostly apart, and she'd also already inherited the house she'd grown up in, so had neither rent nor mortgage.

She was working on consciously erasing all of the awful things her mother used to say to her and trying to replace them with positive thoughts about herself. It was awful even to think it, but at least her mother was no longer around to pick up the emotional abuse right where she'd left off, which was inevitable. Hell, she did it on summer vacations when she came home to stay and work to make money for incidentals at school. It was sad to think that she had very few good memories of the woman who bore her, but that was the truth of the situation.

The struggle not to descend into negativity was very real. And here and now, with pretty much all of the people she'd grown up with in attendance, right on cute—upon seeing him, in particular—all of those old thought patterns and bad habits and bad thinking about herself came roaring back.

She'd let Sheila—who was still her best friend—convince her to come with her to the Ridgeway's annual summer barbeque, and she had regretted it almost immediately.

The Ridgeways didn't have much, but they were always willing to share what they did have with those around them, and thus, literally generations ago, their great-great-grandfather had begun the tradition of getting the townsfolk together at their place and sharing what there was of their wealth. When the latest generation had become orphans at an early age, everyone had assumed that was the last of it.

But the man who was the only reason she could bear to be there had stepped up and let it be known that he and his sister would still love to have the gathering, but that it had to become more of a pot luck than it had been, so they didn't have to try to provide everything. And his friends and neighbors had gladly pitched in, as they'd been doing since the moment two children had found themselves parentless.

It was a big thing every year—the highlight of the summer, always on the 4th of July—and nearly everyone participated, although Jane's mom, of course, couldn't be bothered to go and Roberta Medford's response to her daughter was the same every year when she asked to go.

"Those uppity Ridgeways."

"Uppity?" Jane had asked incredulously. "They're no richer than the rest of us! They're just generous and want everyone to have a good time." She'd wanted to go back then, for no other reason than to surreptitiously watch the big man himself, Elijah, the son and heir. She knew of him— she knew everything she could about him. Despite the death of his beloved parents, he had been captain of the football team, played in a garage band, was a crack shot, and graduated summa cum laude from business school, all while keeping the ranch and what remained of his family with his little sister together.

But she had carefully, deliberately never actually met him. She considered herself to be forgettable enough that, even if she had met him, she would be willing to bet he'd still have no idea she really existed.

And she had no interest in meeting him, either. What

would a blob like herself say to a guy who looked like that? He could have been a celebrity—and he really was the equivalent in their small town. Whatever she said would inevitably embarrass herself or him or both, and then she'd never be able to appear in public again.

No, Jane was very happy just secreting herself into a corner somewhere every year and hopefully never being noticed by anyone—much less by Eli—as her eyes followed him around.

Sheila was her ticket in, always had been.

"Don't you believe that, my girl. Those Ridgeways have land, and land is wealth," her mother had inevitably scoffed during their annual fight when she asked to attend.

"I don't care if they have money or they don't. Sheila's family is going, and they've invited me to come along. It doesn't cost anything, and it'll get me out of your hair for a day." She'd known that those last two things were her aces in the hole.

In the end, her mom had always let her go—although not before she'd made Jane sweat it out, of course.

And now, here she was, years later, doing essentially the same thing she'd always done. While Sheila—who hadn't left town for college but, instead, had stayed at home and found a job in their small town—made the rounds and charmed everyone she spoke to, as usual, she was tucked away from everyone, watching what was going on rather than participating in any of it.

Watching some of what was going on, anyway. Anything that involved Eli was of great interest to her.

His sister had gotten married recently, and her new husband was quite handsy with her in public, walking up to her and popping her hard—and loud—on the tight curve of her shorts in full view of everyone who was standing around talking. She didn't seem to take offense at his action, and neither did anyone else, especially when he pulled her into his arms and gave her a loving, passionate kiss seconds later.

And now, here was Eli, standing disturbingly close to her, suggesting that she could be on the receiving end of such attentions herself.

What could she say to that? To him? She had come to think of herself as relatively glib—her sense of humor had earned her scads of friends in college. But at his inexplicable appearance, her tongue was firmly tied into several knots, and all she could get out was a gross snort she couldn't believe she'd made once it was out of her mouth and a lame, but still heartfelt, "Not friggin' likely."

"Why the hell not?" he asked, sounding genuinely surprised, almost indignant.

When she didn't answer immediately, Eli inadvertently made things a thousand times worse for Jane when he moved around so that he was standing in front of her. "You're Sheila French's friend, aren't you? The two of you went to school with my sister."

"That would be me." Jesus, could she sound any more inane?

"I don't think we've ever been formally introduced. I'm Eli—Eli Ridgeway." He held out an enormous, work worn but clean hand, shaking hers firmly, but with a care for his own strength.

"Jane. Medford," she supplied, glad there was something she could get out of her mouth that didn't make her sound too much like a dolt.

As much as she adored seeing him up close, her nerves were so frazzled because of his proximity that she was worried she was going to faint. Now that he was here, all she wanted was that he should go away, so she could watch him again.

"It's nice to meet you, Jane." He was smiling, of course.

Eli smiled a lot. Then he made the unexpected gesture of touching the tip of his hat to her, surprising the holy hell out of her by leaning against the other side of the same brick column she'd secreted herself behind. Luckily, he was facing the patio and yard, as she was, so at least he wasn't staring right at her.

The house hadn't changed much in all those years, and she'd gravitated to the same bolt hole, having long since determined that this spot gave her the best vantage point from which to watch him, and herself the most cover from which to do so.

Attention in college had been a very different—and much more positive—thing than her experience of attention in her home town, but that comfortable, familiar cloak of insecurities, the fervent wish not to be noticed, especially not by someone like him, was already firmly in place by the time he spoke to her.

"But you didn't answer my question," he interrupted her musings with that sinful voice of his, using the top of his beer to push the brim of his disreputable cowboy hat back, off his forehead, allowing dark blonde, slightly wet ringlets to appear across it.

Jane knew exactly the question to which he was referring, immediately grasping for any other topic.

Literally anything else would do, short of favorite sexual positions or the like.

"Oh, my God, what a cute little dog!"

How had she missed it? She was an animal person. But apparently delicious looking cowboys trumped cute puppies, in some instances.

He dropped down and scooped the itty-bitty thing up in his arms. She hadn't jumped on him, but her tiny body was literally vibrating with excitement when she realized he was going to pick her up.

"This little vixen is Peaches." Eli tucked her securely into his arm, holding her close to his body.

Jane's hand was halfway to the dog before she stopped, knowing that some small dogs could be persnickety. "Is it okay to pet her?"

"Absolutely. She'd love it. She thinks she's terribly neglected by me, because I don't spend all of my day adoring her, as she considers to be her right."

Totally lost in the cuteness, Jane murmured as she petted the dog, who pressed her head eagerly against her hand, "Well, I am in total agreement! How could anyone not want to devote themselves to indulging her every whim?"

She saw the mock withering glance Eli gave her just before he put the dog down again. "I can see that you are a very bad influence. You'll just encourage her in her delusions."

Jane grinned, feeling a bit more at ease than she had moments ago. "Definitely!"

Peaches was incredibly well behaved, though. Once on her feet again, the dog didn't bark or jump up. But she did glue herself to his leg, in a beautiful sitting position, looking slavishly up at him.

You and me, too, sister, Jane couldn't help but think. If she thought she could contort herself into that exact position without risking loss of life, permanent paralysis, dislocation of all of her major joints—or all three at once—she would have been down there herself!

When her eyes left the dog, she suddenly realized how horrible his current position was, because now he was leaning against her column facing her, those big arms crossed over his chest fit to make the buttons on his shirt groan with the effort of covering it. They were outside, and yet there suddenly seemed to be no oxygen available, no matter that she was consciously trying to remind herself to breathe.

Strangely, she didn't have to remind herself not to stare, because she really couldn't even bring herself to so much as look at him, so at least that wasn't a problem.

"I couldn't help noticing, Jane, that you have yet to answer my question, and this is the second time I've had to point that fact out to you. In my book, that would mean you'd already have earned *more* than a loving pop on your beautiful behind."

He couldn't possibly have just said that to her! It was hot and sunny—she must be hallucinating!

Mayday! Mayday! Think of something else to talk about, idiot, and quick!

"Where'd you get her?" she threw out desperately.

"Get who?"

"The dog. Peaches."

"Oh. I rescued her." He took a step closer to her, a crooked finger tipping her chin up so that she had to meet his eyes, although hers were more bouncing off of his then down again. "Stop trying to change the subject, Miss Jane. That'll get you spanked, too."

He *had* said that kind of thing to her! Son of a—

"Sorry. I can't—I think I see my—I gotta go."

She hurried away from him as fast as she could, but she didn't miss him drawling behind her, "It was *very* nice to meet you, Jane Medford."

Holy mother of fu—where the hell was Sheila? Her thoughts were incredibly scattered, and she would swear she could still feel his finger beneath her chin. He'd *touched* her! She had to find her friend and get her to take her home now, immediately. Sooner, if possible.

She found her in the kitchen, talking with Lindsay, Eli's younger sister by about six years, and the very woman who'd gotten her fanny smacked by her husband and, apparently, was totally okay with it.

"Jane!" Lindsay had always been the affectionate type. She wasn't quite one of the cool girls, but she wasn't a pariah, either. Somehow, she'd managed to carve a unique place for herself in the middle somewhere, which was admirable, considering what a social jungle school always was. She was fun and smart and talented and kind to everyone, and everyone liked her.

So, Jane found herself hugged, which wasn't something she was usually okay with, being entirely too body conscious for that, but then, it was over before it began so she just let it happen.

And it felt good! Usually, she just kind of stood there and let someone hug her, enduring it but not reciprocating at all. This time, she brought her hands up and awkwardly patted Lindsay's back.

When she stepped back, Lindsay exclaimed, "Oh my God, your hair is so pretty at that length! Did you cut it while you were away? I wish mine was like yours!"

Jane did her best not to cringe away when Lindsay reached out, casually, to touch it. She'd certainly never thought of her hair as nice. It was just *hair*. She was so busy trying not to move away from the other woman that she didn't answer her at first.

"It's naturally curly, isn't it?"

"Wavy more than curly, but yes. I've never gotten a perm or anything." Her mother would never have spent the money on her. 'Not until you lose the weight', she'd always said. Jane had learned early on not to expect anything nice from her mother without it carrying that particular little devastating—and seemingly unattainable—caveat.

"Mine just hangs there. And the honey blonde is just beautiful, too—compliments your complexion nicely."

Sheila chuckled. "If you don't stop with the compliments, Lindsay, Jane is going to literally shrivel up before our eyes, as if you'd poured water on the Wicked Witch of the West."

Lindsay looked horrified. "Oh, dear, I'm sorry. I didn't mean to make you uncomfortable."

"You didn't," Jane returned. "That's my mother's doing right there."

Lindsay put her arm around Jane, giving her a side hug. "I'm sorry about that! But are you enjoying the party?"

"No," she answered truthfully, watching Lindsay's usual open, smiling face cloud over. Shit! She was not supposed to say that! Say something nice, dummy! "Sorry. Thinking of something else, like the idiot that I am. It's a fantastic party—always is! Thank you guys for putting it on and letting me come! But can I steal Sheila from you for just a moment?"

Jane was asking, but she really wasn't asking, because she already had a death grip on the other girl's hand, and as hard as Sheila tried to retrieve it, she wasn't letting go.

Having never really explored the house at all before, Jane found herself the first open door she could, down the hall off the kitchen, and backed into it, closing the door behind them.

Then she whispered fiercely, "You have got to take me home right this minute! As in now! As in why am I not already in your car!"

Jane made as if to leave the room, expecting that Sheila was going to follow obediently, but she didn't, which meant that Jane had to turn back. "Well?"

"I don't want to go now; we just got here! And besides, Kevin Wilson and Todd Cioffredi have been all over me. If I go, they'll find someone else. Why do you want to leave so soon? What happened?"

What *didn't* happen was an easier question to answer.

Jane bit her lip. "He noticed me."

It took a moment for that sentence to sink in on Sheila's end.

Then her eyes widened and she covered her mouth. "*He* noticed you? *The* he?"

Jane shook her head. "Yeah. *The* he."

"Oh my God—what happened? Tell me everything!"

"What about Kevin and Todd?"

"They'll keep for a minute. I have to hear about this!"

The two of them made themselves comfortable. Jane was a bit reluctant to do so, but Sheila pointed out that the family had to know there would be people wandering through their house today—of all days—and if they'd wanted this room to be off limits, they should have locked it.

So, they sat down, facing each other on a comfortable sofa.

When Jane finished with her tale, Sheila was blown away. "Jesus Christ, he's a spanko, just like you!" she said, making no attempt to lower her voice. "Who'd've thought it?"

"Keep your voice down, for Chrissakes! Or should I go and get a megaphone so you can spill all of my most intimate secrets at once to the entire town?"

It was then that they both heard the door opening, and Jane turned her head to see that the person she least wanted to be at the door was, of course, at the door.

"Oh, I'm sorry," he apologized, pausing politely. "I didn't mean to intrude. I just need to put something in my desk. Old Mrs. Akers gave me a contribution towards the party in lieu of having cooked something, for which I'm sure we are all truly grateful."

Mrs. Akers was a hundred if she was a year, deaf and largely blind, and her food—even when she was young and spry—was wholly unidentifiable as such.

But Jane couldn't be bothered to think about old Mrs. Akers. At that moment, she was busy wishing that she was a wet and dripping bad witch, and then this would all be over in a few seconds.

"That's fine," Sheila smiled, being the only one of the two of them capable of communication.

As he came in and proceeded to rifle through some drawers, Eli said casually, "Sheila, I know my sister was looking for you to help her with something. She's on the patio. I heard Kevin and Todd take your name in vain, too. They're by the pool, or at least they were." He looked up and caught the other girl's eye. "Cindy Hart was headed straight for them, though."

Cindy was incredibly beautiful—tall and thin and lithe, with long, wavy black hair that reached to her mid-back. She was well endowed for a small girl and had nice, slim legs. She was also a notorious skank, and Sheila got up just as Jane grabbed for her and missed completely, backing her way towards the door and trying to silently assure Jane—through some kind of erratic mime-on-acid motions—that everything was going to be okay and motioning for her to stay put.

But Jane knew that if she remained where she was, nothing could be further from the truth, so she, too, got up and headed for the door that Sheila had already closed behind her.

She was so fucking helpful, that one. Jane would deal with her later.

"I wasn't trying to, but I couldn't help overhearing what Sheila said. So, what kind of intimate secrets was she going to tell everyone about in regards to you, Jane? Hmmmm? I have to admit I'm curious." He came about halfway to the door, but no further, standing with his hands on his hips and looking at her all too interestedly.

Oh, holy crap, of course he'd heard that! She could only pray that he hadn't heard the first part of it! Her blush was going to kill her outright one day. "I was just joking. I don't—

don't have any..." Why didn't you quit while you were ahead, stupid? As it was, she had to trail off awkwardly, in barely a whisper. "...intimate secrets."

Eli smiled indulgently at her, but even that couldn't soothe her ragged nerves. She just wanted to live long enough to get out of here.

Finally, as she stood there, Jane forced herself to take a deep breath and then another. It was better just to tell him the truth than to continue with the other thoroughly embarrassing line of questioning. "Sorry to bore you, but I was really just asking Sheila if she'd take me home."

He took another few steps towards her, frowning deeply. "Are you sick or hurt?"

She wanted to say yes to both of them, or at least one of them, but that would have been a lie, and she didn't lie easily —except occasionally to her mother, which she discounted heavily because of the bitching she was so often subjected to.

"Not exactly," Jane admitted reluctantly.

Eli found himself suppressing a smile, not wanting to make her feel any more uncomfortable than she very obviously already did but not really certain how to avoid it, either.

"Good girl for not lying to me, even though you probably wanted to."

Her heart nearly cracked in two at that. Eli Ridgeway, to whom she was a relative stranger, had praised her, something she'd pretty much never gotten from her parental unit. If she hadn't already loved him, that would have done it, right there.

Then he spoiled it, making her literally squeak with his next outrageous statement. "Lying, of course, would definitely have earned you a thorough spanking."

He took the rest of the steps necessary to tower over her

as she stood there with an increasingly horrified look on her face.

"Just so's you know, one spanko to the other," Eli informed her, eyes twinkling brightly as he smiled like the proverbial cat that ate the canary.

Chapter 3

ELI WATCHED while her eyes became saucers.

But then they started to fill with tears as she stood there, apparently struck mute by what he'd said so casually.

He instantly began to castigate himself for being so flip. He should have remembered how she'd reacted just a few moments ago, when she'd practically run from him for teasing her a little about getting a spanking. He hadn't intended to eavesdrop at the door, but he'd been surprised to hear voices coming from the den, which he had mostly taken over so that it could become his study. And he couldn't have been happier about what he heard. But she wasn't having the reaction he'd hoped for at all.

Jane was utterly unprepared for what he did next, taking her hand and guiding her to the sofa, where he encouraged her to sit down. She did so just so that she didn't fall down. Her knees were feeling weak and her heart was going a mile a minute and—of course, right on cue, her eyes filled will tears, nearly to overflowing.

Eli looked at her thoughtfully, and suddenly, he was

lifting her—bodily—onto his lap to hold her tightly in his arms.

It felt like Heaven, but she just couldn't enjoy it. And he shouldn't have done it, either.

"What are you doing?" she asked, immediately struggling to get away, and not getting anywhere for all her attempts.

"You looked as if you were about to cry, so I'm holding you."

"But you shouldn't *lift* me!"

"Why not?" he asked, genuinely curious.

"B-because that's risking grievous bodily harm, and I doubt you want to be in traction for the rest of your life!"

He looked around at himself, not letting her go. "Do I look like picking you up has hurt me in any way? Do I look like I'm in agony?" His potent gaze was back resting on her, where she least wanted it to be. Then he set her nerves —in parts of her she would rather not acknowledge owning at the moment—to jangling again by confessing huskily, "I can assure you that pain is the *last* thing I'm feeling at this moment, with you sitting so prettily on my lap."

She forced herself to ignore him—and the very prominent evidence she could feel beneath her that he was telling the truth, as well as the provocative things he was saying—in her fervor to get free. "I shouldn't b-be on your lap, either. I'll br-break your legs or c-cut off the circulation to them at the very least."

"Stop."

It was the quiet, calm way he said it that got her to do exactly that.

"I take it you're saying that it's your weight that's going to cause all of those things to happen?" he asked gently.

Embarrassed to the tips of her toes and the split ends of her hair, Jane nodded, looking down, unable to speak through the tears that were darkening her shirt in large splotches.

"Well, rest assured, then, that isn't something you need to think about in regards to me. I am perfectly fine, and you are exactly where you should be." He paused, adding, "You're where I *want* you to be, or I wouldn't have put you there."

She shook her head vehemently back and forth, tears still rolling down her face.

To her surprise, he produced a little pocket packet of Kleenex. By the way of explanation, he told her, "You may or may not know it, but my mom and dad died while I was still in high school and Linds was in grade school. I adore her. I mean, I love that girl to death," he admitted without a trace of embarrassment. "But she cries. Quite a bit. When she's happy, when she's sad, when she's frustrated or angry. I can't stand her tears—unless they're happy ones—but I got into the habit long ago of carrying around a bit of Kleenex so I could dry her tears and let her blow her nose and help her feel a bit better while I hugged her tight—just like I'm doing with you right now—and tried to pry out of her what was going on that made her feel bad."

Damn—the man was a fucking awesome brother, too! Jesus, was there nothing he was horrible at? His goddamned perfection was yet another reason—not that she needed any more than she already had—why she shouldn't be where she was at the moment.

"But Lindsay's skinny. And you're her brother—a very good brother," she ventured tremulously. "She belongs on your lap."

Jane made another attempt to get off him, but he simply held onto her, and there she sat, until he decided to let her go, apparently.

"Well, she *is* my sister, so there's a bit of an inherent right there, I guess," he said sagely, but his tone became a bit harder as he continued. "But I'll have you know that I don't let just anyone sit on my lap."

Jane almost peeped up at him at that, but she couldn't quite convince herself to do so.

But it was his next words that had her looking up to stare at him, open mouthed, as he delivered them in a calm but mildly stern voice.

"And you had better never let me catch you uttering so much as another negative word about your weight around me, Jane Medford, or the spanking I was teasing you about earlier is going to become a reality that I can *promise* will make you severely regret whatever it was you said."

He couldn't help but grin at those incredibly shocked blue eyes when her head snapped up, with their heavy fringe of dark, wet lashes around them. She was incredibly cute, but she obviously didn't feel that way about herself.

As soon as she recovered from the shock enough to realize that Eli was looking back at her, she lowered her eyes, but he caught her chin on the way down and brought them back to his.

"L-let me go, please," she whispered.

"I will, Jane. I have guests to see to out there, although I'd much rather stay in here and give you a very thorough spanking, then hold you in my arms—just like this—as you cry it out. Maybe you'd even let me make it up to you," he suggested with an audacious wink, watching her blush beautifully. "I would certainly like to get the opportunity to convince you to do that."

He let go of her chin, and her gaze drifted downward again, until she was staring at her hands in her lap.

"You came here with Sheila, didn't you? You two usually come here together. I remember seeing you before."

That was a truly terrifying thought, but she nodded in agreement.

"And," he ventured in a whisper, "I'd bet you were trying to convince her to take you home because of what I'd said to you earlier that sent you skittering away from me, weren't you, baby?"

She started to shake her head, not wanting to confirm what he already seemed to intuit about her with eerie accuracy.

"Jane."

Her shaking head became a nodding one really quickly at that tone.

"That's another way to earn a spanking from me. And not just a spanking, either. Lying to me will get you my belt singing across your backside, and I promise you, it won't be the only thing singing."

His arms melted from around her, and she—contrarian that she was—felt the loss of his warmth and safety quite acutely.

But before she could escape, he pulled her down to capture her lips in a very unexpected, incredibly sensual kiss that left her breathless when he raised his head to look down at her with a smoldering look.

The errant though ran through her head that his beard wasn't prickly against her skin at all as she had imagined it would be, but was rather soft, adding yet another sexy element to that sweet intimacy.

Then he stood with her in his arms and let her down onto her feet slowly, as if to prove to her that lifting her didn't cause him any kind of injury whatsoever. But mostly because he loved the feel of her sliding down his body and rubbing against a cock that was causing his zipper to bulge embarrassingly.

"I take it Sheila declined to take you home?"

"Yes," Jane answered quietly, looking down, as was her habit.

That was one he would correct right quick, given the chance.

And Eli intended that he would be given that chance. He'd take it, if he had to, but he'd much prefer that she would come to give herself to him. That was his real goal.

"I'm glad. I suppose I should do the gentlemanly thing and take you home, myself, but I'd much rather show you a better time, in hopes that you'll wanna hang around." He took her hand in his, covering the back with his own so that hers was sandwiched between them, and she was utterly lost in the warm safety he was providing. "Would you be my date this evening, Miss Jane?" he asked with a lazy grin. Hoping to pre-empt the immediate "no" he knew instinctively that she wanted to give him, he added, "I'll take you home whenever you say, so that you're not dependent on Sheila if you want to go, but I want you to give me an hour of your time —right now—to try to convince you to stay."

Jane snatched her hand back, and his remained there for a few seconds after he'd let it go, as if missing the feel of her like she'd missed his arms around her. "I-I can't do that, but thank you."

"Why not, little one?"

That got her to actually glare at him, her angry eyes colliding with his clear green ones. "You shouldn't call me that."

"Why not?" he asked patiently, clasping his hands in front of him and adopting the manspreading stance to beat all manspreading stances.

Her eyes had already wandered away from his, and he brought them back. He saw another flash of anger at his insistence, but it was gone very quickly. Most men would have missed it. "Be-because it's not true. I'm not little, and it's ridiculous to call me that."

He took a step towards her, his arm shooting out to stop

her from taking one back. He didn't hug her or pull her to him, but he did keep her right where he wanted her.

"It's true from where I'm standing. You're a good foot shorter than I am, at least. That makes you little."

"That doesn't take into consideration my fat ass."

She wasn't looking at him anymore, and he didn't say anything for a bit, but when he finally did, she heartily wished he hadn't.

"Oh, honey, what did I just say you shouldn't do?" he asked her with a terrible, regretful calm that was threaded with steel, his head tilted just a bit as he gazed down at her.

She was literally babbling at the thought of what she knew he intended to do.

"But you can't—you're not going to—you wouldn't, would you?"

While at the same time, her flesh was weak—very, very weak—and it definitely wanted him to do exactly what he'd said he'd do. She hadn't meant for this to happen in any way —hadn't plotted to get him to do it. What she'd said was the result of a lifetime spent carefully honing that exact reflex. It was always better to insult herself than to hear someone else do it, so she always tried to get there first.

And there was also the very valid—if frightening—idea that this was definitely going to be the only time she would ever be near him—hell, probably any guy at all—in this capacity or otherwise, and she knew she could live on the memories of it for the rest of her life.

As much as it conspired against her in some ways, the majority of her mind was utterly horrified at the thought, though, growing more so by the second when he turned quickly and locked the door, then corralled her over to the unfortunately nearby arm of the couch before she could collect her scattered thoughts enough to put up much of a defense.

She didn't even know how he'd done it, but she suddenly found herself bent over it, her face in the cushion she'd just been sitting on.

He was standing to one side, by the back of the couch, with one hand on her mid-back. And that, apparently, was all he needed. Try as she might, she couldn't get up.

"This is a very cute sundress, and it fits you perfectly. Have I already told you that?"

It was a conversational gambit that she didn't expect, but Jane was much too preoccupied with what he was doing to her at the moment, so his question went unanswered as she tried to come to grips with where she found herself.

The first spank she'd ever received in her life was from him, seconds later. It was everything she'd ever thought it would be, but it was nothing like she'd thought it would be, at the same time. The pain made her catch her breath. And that was just one!

She might not have known him well—or really at all—stalking him occasionally but compulsively not withstanding —but she had an idea that he wasn't the type to stop there.

"Jane, I think I've already told you what I expect in regards to be answered promptly."

She found herself embarrassingly motivated to provide him with exactly the response he wanted to hear.

"No, you didn't say anything to me about my dress."

"Good girl," he praised with gentle warmth.

Oh. My. God. She could so easily become addicted to hearing that phrase from him! He was even more dangerous to her sanity than she'd originally thought!

"It's the truth. I know you probably don't—and maybe can't right now—believe me, but you look extremely fetching."

She didn't snort in disbelief as she definitely would have before she found herself in this situation—she was learning, although apparently not quickly enough to save herself from what was to come.

His palm covered her rear end in a not so subtle threat. "Now, little girl, I know that your mother taught you what to say when someone compliments you," he chided.

More excruciating endearments!

And she wasn't about to get into her mother with him. "Th-thank you."

"You're welcome," accompanied by bottom pats.

While she was silently squealing about those, and she knew she was crazy for saying so, she still couldn't hold it back. Might's well get as much of her weirdness out as possible. It wasn't as if this was going to develop into any kind of relationship. "I don't like compliments. I don't get many of them, but wh-when someone says s-something nice about me, it just makes me want to disappear."

That hand moved up a bit to rub her lower back. "I know, honey, and that's just horribly wrong."

She wasn't trying to get away, but suddenly, she wanted to see his eyes, and as she craned her head up, he met hers warmly.

Jane opened her mouth to say something else, but his dark eyebrow went up.

"Be careful of what you say. Consider the position you're already in."

Eli watched her face fall, and that told him all he needed to know. She had, indeed, been going to say something else that was self-hating, and he wasn't going to let her do it. If she said something like that within his hearing, she could always expect to find herself put back into this position. Or maybe over his lap, he mused. Or the back of the couch. Or, even better, pillows on his bed.

But he was getting away from himself. She was here, in front of him, bent over the arm of the couch in his den. And he knew, from the happy accident of his unintentional eaves-dropping—that she shared his exact tastes.

"Has anyone else ever spanked you?"

"My mom when I was little, but I have no memory of it," she answered truthfully.

"I meant any lovers, anybody you've played with?"

Her "no" was a bit clipped, but he put it down to a first timer's nerves. He knew this was hardly where she expected to end up today.

It had been on the tip of Jane's tongue to say, "What lovers?" but she managed not to.

"Well, I've spanked a few women in my time, usually in regards to a punishment, because they allowed me to guide them in their lives while we were together and correct them when I felt that was necessary. Some of them I spanked, also, because I knew they got a lot of pleasure from it."

What was she supposed to say to that?

"Oh."

Did he just chuckle?

"Okay, I'll stop trying to get you to talk about this, but don't think I'm not going to want to discuss this very subject with you in the future, because I can guarantee you that I will."

Future? What future? Jane wondered, but not for long.

The man was incredibly strong—he had to be to have picked her up—and it showed every time his hand came in contact with her butt. In her fantasies, her spanker always bared her bottom, but the reality of the situation was that she was exceedingly grateful that he hadn't done that! It was definitely bad enough with the meager defense of her panties and the light cotton dress she was wearing.

She had thought it would be a short, sharp thing—a couple swats and it would be over. But it went on for much longer than that. The burning sting she felt with each smack became overwhelming and he showed absolutely no signs of stopping.

He covered every inch of her bottom and then some very methodically, reaching down to the tops of her thighs, which had her trying to dance those targets away from him in a move that she couldn't imagine looked any too graceful, to no further up her back then a couple of finger widths above the generous crest of her backside.

Jane had promised herself she wouldn't cry, but that was a futile vow. She'd been hiccoughing sobs and breathing raggedly through tears since a humiliatingly short amount of time after he started!

Eli was watching her carefully as he punished her. It was a bit of a harder correction than she might have warranted, technically, especially considering that this was her first time. But he wanted to make sure she realized that the next time that awful habit she had of putting herself down reared its head, he expected her not to give voice to what she'd probably spent her lifetime saying about herself.

It seemed to be automatic for her to do that—something she didn't even think about, really—but he intended to help her break that habit, if he had to roast her backside red each and every day.

He knew that tears had come to her early on, and he wasn't sure whether it was just the newness of the situation, or if she was truly that sensitive. If he got other chances to punish her—which he certainly intended to—he'd learn more about how she dealt with it. Some women never, ever cried, some cried and begged and pleaded from before he'd even touched them. She seemed to fall somewhere in between, which was just about right, as far as he was concerned.

He stopped when he stopped—he wasn't looking or waiting for any particular point or reaction from her. Eli tried to keep a general idea of how long the punishment was taking in his head and fit it to the crime. As offenses went, he'd categorize this as medium naughty. He knew that others might consider it to be a lower priority, but he really did not like to hear her talking about herself that way. He would have decked any man he'd heard saying things like that about her, so he wasn't about to put up with it from her.

It seemed to Jane that he went from swatting her unbearably hard, to tugging her relatively limp, unwieldy body into his arms and onto his lap again and holding her there, the same hand that had been spanking her now holding her face to his chest as his big thumb brushed her damp cheek soothingly. And she let him—she let him hold and comfort her. She was too blank, too mindless to object, floating on some odd feeling she didn't have a name for. Her butt hurt like a bitch, but that didn't seem to matter. She felt calm and whole, in a way she never had before.

Eli moved just a bit away from her, and she surprised him very pleasantly by cuddling up to him. "Shhh. I'm not going to let go." What he did, instead, was lean down to kiss away the tears that were still making their way—if more sluggishly than before—down her cheeks. She was sniffling quite delicately, and he found it, and everything about her, enchanting. Eli didn't stop himself from bending down to kiss her once, quite tentatively, then, when she didn't object in any way whatsoever, he pressed his lips to hers again, more passionately, his hand coming up to cradle her head with infinite gentleness.

It didn't remain there, though, and as she felt it caress down over her body, he murmured against her ear, "If you tell me to stop, Jane, I will, immediately. But don't. I'll make it worth your while not to."

Although she tried to squirm away, he wouldn't allow it. In fact, he kept her eyes locked with his as his hand found its way beneath the hem of her dress. "You know what to say to end this if you want to, but until I hear that word, I'm going to dedicate myself to one thing—your pleasure."

She jumped a bit as he found the juncture of her thighs, not really processing what he was saying or doing. He hadn't even touched anything particularly important yet, and she thought she was going to climax without him ever having to do so.

She knew she should have been more forceful about getting away from him, should have said "Stop!" loud and clear, but she didn't really want to. What he was doing felt dangerously good to her, and as long as he continued to move as slowly and carefully as he was, she wasn't going to be able to convince herself to say the magic word.

Seconds later, he moved the crotch of her panties aside to find her warmth. Jane arched herself into his hand, knowing she should have been doing the exact opposite, and he nibbled her ear. "Patience, Jane," he scolded mildly, in the perfect way, and she again nearly came right then.

He used only one finger, but that was more than talented enough to accomplish his goal. Eli deliberately slid his middle finger down through her soft seam, parting her folds steadily around it, and barely able to contain himself when he found so much ample evidence of just how passionate she was.

He could hardly believe it!

Then he pulled his dripping fingertip back the way it had come, to find what he really wanted already swollen and throbbing and eagerly awaiting his touch.

Jane clutched at his shirt as if in distress.

"Shhhhh," he soothed. "Let me do this for you, Jane. I want to see you come for me."

Almost before he finished the command, he was doing just that. He was amazed at how quickly it had happened—

most women took quite a bit more time than that, in his experience. Jane twisted and writhed and arched and moaned as he continued to stroke her, not letting up until she had had a second and a third climax.

"Son of a bitch, that was hot!" he breathed as he pressed his lips to her damp temple, holding her still when she would have gotten up. "No, stay with me," he whispered, his hand still cupping her between her legs, feeling her continuing to contract beneath his fingers.

Jane, who was only really pushing herself to do so because she thought she should, let go of the idea of escape and allowed herself to bask in his attentions as he kissed here and touched there while helping her down from her incredible high, letting long moments pass as he held her.

But their sensual interlude was interrupted by an unmistakable sound—tiny nails scratching persistently against the door.

Jane found herself kissed reverently on the forehead then very reluctantly lifted off his lap and placed very carefully onto the couch next to him. Even with his gentleness, she ended up moving to lean on her hip rather than actually sit normally. "I imagine your behind is still quite sore," he said, watching her maneuver herself into that more comfortable position with no small amount of satisfaction.

She had no idea what came over her, especially considering everything that had just happened between them, but she found herself smacking his shoulder sharply.

But he just smiled, then he schooled his handsome features into a big, bad frown, warning darkly, "Now, if you ever hit me and I find out about it, little girl…" which earned him a smile.

He ducked into an adjacent bathroom and washed his hands. Then, as Peaches was at least as dedicated to her own task as he had been to his, he strode over to the door and let her in.

"Interrupted in my romantic pursuits by my own damned dog!" he said disgustedly as he leaned down to pick her up while she literally danced at his feet, which set her into a frenzy of ecstatic licking as he petted her. "My sister is her next favorite person. Lindsay must have gotten busy and forgotten to keep track of her."

Eli stood in front of Jane, the dog in one arm as he extended his other hand to her. "Shall we go out and mingle?"

His chest hurt when she began to fidget with her fingers in her lap, looking very uncomfortable. "Give me your hand, babygirl."

Jane knew she would never, ever tire of hearing him call her that.

She did so, very tentatively, finding herself held tightly to his other side as his arm slid naturally around her waist.

And that voice—even fully satisfied as she was, he could have gotten her to jump off a cliff if he'd just told her to in that incredibly addictive tone, which lay in some sexy middle ground between cajoling and ordering. The truth was that he'd said to her the same things that others had said to her— although not in the same type of situation. But for some reason, it rang truer—she believed it more—coming from him. Perhaps it was because he said it with the absolute conviction of someone who wouldn't hesitate to back up what he was saying.

His demeanor was strong and calming, his words deep and reassuring. "There's nothing to be nervous about, Jane. It's all folks you know, who know you. And I'll be right at your side the entire time. You keep a hold of me if you get anxious. But you don't have to talk to anyone—beyond generic politeness—or do anything that you don't want to, I promise."

"Does that mean I can go home now?" she asked pertly, and he had to grin because she looked so damned pleased with herself.

"No, little miss. It means that I'm claiming my hour, and then we'll reassess."

Another longer, even slower, kiss was bestowed upon her, his open mouth slanting over hers this time, with him pulling back at the end of it to give her a look that nearly sizzled the already wet panties right off of her!

"Damn, woman!" he groaned. "We'd better leave now or I'm going to carry you to my room, put you beneath me on my bed, and see how long it takes me to make you scream."

Chapter 4

NEEDLESS TO SAY, she hadn't left in an hour. Or even two hours. Although he'd surprised—and delighted—her by actually addressing the limit he'd set. Some men might have simply ignored it, but exactly one hour later, Eli had stopped cold dead and turned to her—they were strolling lazily around the place together and he was showing her the roses he had taken up growing, in his father's place—and gave her a considering look out of the side of his eye as he gathered her to him. "Hour's up. Want me to take you home?"

She really wanted to say yes because she didn't think his ego needed feeding. "Maybe?" she teased.

His eyebrow went up, although he was half-smiling, too, glad that she felt comfortable enough to tease him. "I'm afraid that's not one of the choices. Yes or no, little lady."

She thought it was a strange choice for him to pat her bottom at this particular moment, but he did.

As usual, she was contemplating her feet when she answered him at a deliberately low pitch. "No," she whispered, knowing he couldn't hear her.

Although he was elated that she wanted to stay, he

wanted a bit more from her than that. "That ain't gonna cut it, either, I'm afraid. When you answer me, or when you tell me good or bad news, or when you confess that you've done something naughty, I want you to look me in the eye, Jane. I want you to always do that, but I know it's very hard for you to do, so I'll start with those situations."

It took her a minute, and he didn't get mad, but he did tighten his arms around her as if willing her his support and strength. Finally, biting her lip nearly through, she found his eyes. "No, I don't want to go home. I want to stay here, with you, please."

He kissed the top of her head. "And so you shall stay right here, where you belong."

In fact, she'd outlasted Sheila, who had given her the thumbs up as she'd left with Todd and Kevin.

It ended up that she—like Peaches—had barely left his side the entire time. He'd been phenomenal, making sure she was included in everything she wanted to do, not that that was much, really, so he'd just included her on his own rounds as host. He'd taken possession of her hand or kept it tucked into his elbow almost the entire time. They'd moved casually from group to group, and everyone greeted him enthusiastically, of course. Eli did his best to draw her into conversations, just small talk, really, among people of long acquaintance.

He wasn't very successful at his attempts, but he didn't push her about it, not being sure if she was truly shy, or if she was just self-conscious, or if she was shy because she was self-conscious, or vice versa. It didn't matter to him what the cause was. He just wanted her to feel at ease and have a good time.

It wasn't until they mosied over to a group of people who greeted her warmly before they greeted him that she perked up considerably. It took him a minute to put it together, but then it struck him. They were teachers. Almost everyone from the principal on down was in attendance.

"You looking forward to September?" Al Ketcham, the assistant principal, had asked her.

And she had lit up. He thought she'd probably even forgotten that he was beside her. And he was surprised and totally charmed at how animated and engaged she was, talking about something she obviously loved to do.

"Oh, yes! I've been researching and working on bulletin boards and making lesson plans for math—"

"I can tell you haven't been teaching long, youngster! The first day of school is a four-letter word after about the first year!" Alice Hough, who was old enough to have taught pretty much everyone at that shindig, crowed.

Jane's face fell, which made Eli want to do say something he shouldn't to the nasty Miss Hough, but then first grade teacher, Mary Hubbard, got up and patted her arm. "Don't you listen to her, Jane. She's always like that. There are plenty of us around who still enjoy it, and I know you will, too. You always were one to want to help me in class. I'm so glad we got you to come back here and teach!"

Eli watched Jane color brightly and squeezed her hand where it still lay on his arm. "So am I!"

"You feel free to come to me with any questions, but I bet Aileen Sutter will be more than willing to help you, too. She's home with the gout, poor thing, but she'll be better by then."

Aileen was the other fourth grade teacher. They really didn't need two fourth grade teachers, so Jane had been brought on with an eye to Aileen probably retiring in not too long.

"Thank you, Mrs. Hubbard!"

"You can call me Mary, dear. I know it's hard to remember, but you're not a student any longer."

They drifted away from that group and were on their own. "Are you hungry?"

"No, thank you." It was her rote response to eating in public around strangers, and eating in public in front of him made it even more so than usual.

Eli looked puzzled. "No? Really? Don't you like barbecue?"

In truth, she loved it—entirely too much than was good for her! If it was slathered in sweet, molasses sauce, she'd eat pretty much anything! But she couldn't bring herself to do so in front of all of these people, who were certain to be silently judging the size of the plate she took, which would force her to take only salad, and precious little of that, too.

And now there was Eli's opinion on her food choices to take into consideration, too—well ahead of everyone else's.

So, it always boiled down to just being better not to eat at all. She'd wait and eat when she got home. It was what she was used to doing in this type of situation, anyway. Jane didn't think she'd ever eaten anything while she was here—at least, not once she'd hit puberty.

And it certainly wasn't as if she was going to starve to death if she spent a few hours not eating. But she couldn't say any of that to him, of course.

"I'm feeling a little queasy. Nerves, I guess." She looked down then up at him deliberately, and he seemed to forget entirely about wanting her to eat, for a moment at least. She'd never developed any wiles at all—never had the chance to. But that certainly was an interesting reaction that was poking rather forcefully into her tummy. Jane filed it away for further consideration at a time when he wasn't holding her so distractingly close.

It earned her a short, hard kiss that thrilled her to her core—which was still thrumming in the aftermath of his caresses.

"Well, I'm starving. Do you mind?"

He seemed serious about the question, which confused her. "Of course not!"

Eli scoured the patio and found a nice table for them, guiding her there. "If you'll just sit tight for a moment, I'll be right back." He took a step away then came back. "You're sure you're okay if I eat in front of you? It won't make you feel sicker?"

That gave her a huge twinge of guilt for lying to him, but it was better than the alternative.

"No, it won't. You go get what you want."

Her guilt was somewhat assuaged when he said in a terribly dominant way, "Don't move," before heading to the heaped tables of food as if he thought it would all be gone before he got there, elbowing his way into the line amongst some of his longtime male friends who all laughed and elbowed him right back.

Lovely. Now they were going to tease him about hanging around with her. Well, it had been nice while it lasted.

Suddenly, Sheila sat down in the chair that was supposed to be Eli's. "Oh my gawd!!" she squealed in a hushed but urgent whisper, bouncing up and down in the chair, which was something Jane would never have dared to do.

"And you don't even know the half of it! I cannot believe it! What the hell is happening? Is this an alternate universe, or what?"

"If it is, I hope it never ends for you! I wanna hear all the juicy details tomorrow!" She popped up as quickly as she'd sat down, leaning over to say before she departed, "I have a couple of my own on the line." Then she patted Jane's shoulder and left in search of them.

"Juicy" was right, Jane thought, shifting in her chair for many more reasons than the usual she'd encountered when she was stalking him.

"I hope I didn't drive Sheila away," he said when he sat down next to her with not one but two plates full of food, almost all of them things she would have loved to have eaten —Merrill Denny's famous fried chicken, Jill Pickering's potato salad, and a heap of his own secret recipe barbecued brisket, not to mention a slab of homemade apple pie as big as his head. And it didn't help that she was hungry! Jane hadn't eaten since lunch and it was five o'clock, and despite what a lot of their detractors seemed to think, fat people did need to eat, just like anyone else.

He even tried to offer her some of it, but apparently, her hungry look resembled her sick look, because he laid off doing that after only a couple of attempts.

Throughout the rest of the afternoon and evening, though, he would ask her—so solicitously—every once in a while, if she was feeling better.

It made Jane sigh at deceiving him every time, but under all the guilt, she couldn't help but be feel secretly amazed at how wonderfully he was treating her.

As they were heading into evening, he volunteered her to help Lindsay with getting all the food taken care of, which she really didn't mind at all. Jane was very happy to help in any way she could, and the women of the town—having grown up doing this and being taught about it by their mothers and their mother's mothers—were extremely organized and knew exactly how it worked best so that the Ridgeways weren't left with any kind of mess.

In fact, she got very caught up in that until he found her more than an hour later, tugging her away from the gaggle of females and bringing her back outside with him, which his sister, indulgently, didn't seem to mind too much.

In the meantime, while she had been slaving away, the sun set and lights of all kinds—holiday lights and regular, some stolen from trailer awnings, everyone brought what they could—were all strung up and turned on, and the place looked like a fairyland. Normally, she was long gone by now, but she'd been missing a lot in leaving so early! Everyone who cared to had also brought their instruments, and some couples were dancing where the tables had been cleared and moved to create room for just that.

Eli wasn't shy. They'd found their way back to a hexagonal table with what she noticed were sturdy benches surrounding it and were just about to sit and enjoy some homemade lemonade. He had made sure—by keeping hold of her arm—that she was pressed tight up against his side, before he turned to ask, "Will you dance with me?"

Her first look was awe, for some reason he didn't understand, but that was quickly chased away and her expression literally closed up while he watched it happen, with not a small amount of sadness.

"No, thank you," came her subdued answer. "I don't dance."

Well, she could dance, but she didn't dance, not in front of anyone, anyway. That was yet another lie—she figured he'd be a stickler enough to think that semantics counted—she felt trapped into telling him, and his caution against doing so rang through her head as she did it. The truth was that she learned dance steps and routines very easily. She'd never had lessons, but Sheila had, and she'd taught Jane how to do them, and Jane did them better than she did, by a long shot.

"You don't dance, or you won't dance?"

"Yes."

He had to chuckle at that. "All right, I'll let you get away with it this time, but you owe me one."

"Don't hold your breath," she muttered.

"I won't, Janey. But be forewarned, I usually get what I want, in the end."

Janey. No one had ever called her that!

His parents had had lights installed in and around the pool so that Eli and Lindsay could swim at night if they wanted to. He couldn't convince her to swim, either, but she had a better excuse for that—she hadn't brought a bathing suit, he'd been sorry to discover.

But he didn't push her about that, either. "Well, the next time you're here, you'll have to bring one."

Jane smiled at Eli, not about to go any further with that whole land mine of a subject.

Overall, though, she could see cloud nine in the rear-view mirror!

Of course, she knew that something was going to come along and ruin it—most likely that he was going to come to his senses shortly—but she was storing up so many memories! She couldn't even contemplate the sexual ones, yet—that had been so incredibly unexpected! She was still working on coming to grips with the more normal stuff. Like, he didn't seem to mind her looking at him all the time as if he hung the moon, and he did enough of his own looking, too, constantly making her blush with it. Eventually, he was going to get bored with her, obviously, since there were so many things he wanted to do but she wouldn't.

But it was still the happiest time of her life, bar none!

The fact that she was being a stick in the mud didn't seem to bother him in the least. When they sat down, he planted his elbow in the table next to her and tucked her up against the front of him, his other hand resting lightly on her tummy and making her clit jump even from that distance.

And she didn't even bother to try to move it, either! She knew he would have no idea of just how monumental that was for her, but it was. If he didn't want it there, it wouldn't be there; of that she was quite sure.

Of course, that also meant that she was spending her

time trying to keep her gut sucked in, which was supremely uncomfortable, but so worth it.

The music was great. There were a ton of very talented people in town, so they just sat there and listened together, sometimes both of them singing along with everyone else to a familiar song. Since he'd been in a band—and had kept up his interest in music—he always let everyone use whatever instruments he had on hand, and the townsfolk brought their own banjoes, guitars, and, in one case, even an autoharp, and everybody—of every skill level—just played.

At one point, one of his bandmates had offered him one of his own acoustic guitars, but he declined, shaking his head and putting his arms more fully around Jane. "No, thanks. I'm very happy with what I already have in my arms."

That got a chorus of "aws" from the people around them and set Jane's face to blazing. She was very happy that it was quite dark in the shadows where they were, but Eli didn't miss a trick.

"I love it when you blush."

"I blush all the time!"

"I know! It's incredibly cute!"

She yawned then, trying to hide it from him from pure instinct. She had a feeling that, if he saw it, he was likely to suggest that they end the evening, and she never wanted it to end.

"I saw that, little one."

"No, you didn't!" she returned instantly. "It was a figment of your imagination, I swear." Jane held her hand up as if she was taking an oath.

"Uh huh. I don't think so, and I don't think you want to fib to me, either, do you? Or did I not make a firm enough point earlier?"

His hands were trying to surreptitiously squeeze her

bottom, and if he hadn't held her tight, she would have rock-eted off the seat.

"You weren't feeling well earlier, either," he said, as if that was the deciding factor for him. "Do you need to find Sheila and let her know you have a ride?"

Jane grumbled wordlessly, secretly loving that he was taking such good care of her, but replied, "No, she left earlier because I told her that you would bring me home." She'd worried about that a bit at the time, but not now.

"Good. Then let's get you home."

He stood first, but kept her hand in his, then helped her up.

Those who weren't playing noticed that they were leaving and called their goodbyes. Eli was in the process of leading her around to the side of the house, where there was a gate that led to the driveway and his car, when she stopped suddenly.

"Wait! I want to say thank you for having me to Lindsay before I go." Jane'd always made a habit of that, even when she hadn't had Lindsay's handsome hunk of a brother at her side, and she didn't want to forget her manners now that she did—at least temporarily, anyway.

He let her go, but reluctantly, following after her as she hurriedly made her way into the kitchen, where she thought Lindsay probably still was, trailing behind her like Peaches trailed loyally after him.

Jane had been right, and Lindsay had thanked her right back for her help then hugged her again, and this time, Jane hugged her right back. That was the scene that greeted Eli's eyes, and he was very grateful for it. He was glad that Lindsay liked Jane, because he intended that she would be seeing a lot more of her in the future.

"All right, Jane, c'mon, we're outta here. She was feeling a bit under the weather a little earlier," he explained to his sister, "and I think she needs to go home and go to bed."

"Oh, I'm sorry to hear that!" Lindsay then asked him a very innocent, normal question that made Jane snort, then cough as if she belonged in a TB ward to cover it up. "Will you be coming back home?"

Eli had noticed that she had already drifted away from him—deliberately so, after his sister's presumptive question. And now Jane was actively trying to slip on by him. But Eli could talk and chew gum at the same time, so, as she did, his hand shot out and caught her wrist.

"Yes, I will be home tonight, Linds. Thanks ever so much for asking. You are absolutely no help in this endeavor at all."

She looked unrepentant as she grinned up at her brother. "Always glad to be of service!"

Eli growled as Jane bit the tongue that was sticking slightly out of her mouth while she diligently tried to pry his fingers off her wrist while he wasn't looking.

Unfortunately for her, he was now looking.

"You can try all you like, honey, but my fingers won't budge until I want them to," he informed her as he began to walk, and, by sheer necessity, she did too.

"He's right—take it from me!" Lindsay called after them. "But if you bite him hard enough—he'll let you go!"

"You keep your advice to yourself, or I'll tell Jake on you," he growled back to her. To Jane, he warned, "Considering the current condition of your backside, I wouldn't suggest you attempt that."

"About what?" Lindsay called.

"Oh, any number of infractions I can think of," came the smug threat from her big brother.

Then they both heard her subdued, "Dammit!"

But she rallied, because the unmistakable sounds of an enthusiastic Bronx Cheer being given followed them out to his car, an ancient sedan that had to have seen much better days. Or not. If she could remember correctly—and she could—it was given to him by his grandfather when he turned sixteen, and it wasn't young then, either. But Eli could —and did—keep pretty much anything mechanical going for as long as possible. He wasn't cheap—this party was irrefutable evidence of that—but he was careful with his money, and that wasn't at all a bad thing, as far as she was concerned.

The ride home was an incredible cap to what had been —for her, anyway—a fairy tale—okay, and part porno— afternoon and evening. She knew she was going to wake up tomorrow and have turned into one of the ugly stepsisters, to distort that particular fairy tale, but that was fine. She'd really lived out a dream scenario with him—well, they hadn't slept together and they hadn't gotten married, but close enough— and she had accepted its inevitably short duration from the beginning, having never expected it, or anything even vaguely resembling it, to happen in the first place.

He had put her into the car and fastened her seatbelt for her—which she had tried not to let him do. But he had given her a look that had had her releasing her death grip on the belt without even thinking about not doing so.

Then he'd come around and gotten in, taking her hand back in his as if it was something he did out of long habit. "Sorry about the quality of the ride."

"Why?" she asked him in all honesty. "Do you think I drive a Maserati?"

Eli laughed at that. Her attitude was refreshing. He'd had women look down on him when he arrived in this car— sometimes deliberately, sometimes not—to pick them up for a date. Those were some of the ones who didn't get second dates.

"Radio?"

"Okay."

"Or CD?"

"Radio's fine."

"Care what station?"

"No, put on whatever you'd usually listen to."

He gave her a considering glance, but she meant it. She could have asked him to play oldies—since that's all her mom let her listen to while she was growing up, and they had grown on her, kind of like mold. But it would give her much more information about him if she let him pick for himself.

"You sure?"

"Yeah, definitely," she agreed, just praying it wasn't going to be talk radio or opera.

"You might not like it."

"I have relatively eclectic tastes in music. I'll be fine. Besides, it's not a three-day road trip to my house."

He punched his favorite station and she recognized it as the one she listened to, herself. Oldies.

"So there'd be a fight if we were on a three-day road trip?"

"No, we'd both compromise. Half the time what you like, half the time what I did."

"Sounds fair enough." He maneuvered them from the long dirt road that was his driveway onto the long dirt road that was an actual highway. "What do you like for music?"

Jane laughed, and his cock became uncomfortably rigid at the sound, for some reason. Perhaps because she didn't laugh very often and he found the sound incredibly sexy. "Oldies."

He had to smile. "Well, I already knew we were compatible in a couple of very important areas, but it's nice to know that there are others we can enjoy in public, too."

"Stop!"

Jane thought he'd continue teasing her mercilessly, but he

didn't. Instead, he said very earnestly, "I'm glad you came with Sheila today. I know it must've been out of your comfort zone."

She was surprised he knew what a comfort zone was! "I come every year."

"I know."

There was a wealth of information just in those two words, so much so that she couldn't really even contemplate it right now.

They were at her place long before she wanted to be.

"Got you home before you turned in a pumpkin," he announced, not understanding why she was laughing as he helped her out of the car. "What's so funny?"

"That's not how the fairy tale goes, either!"

"It's not? And what do you mean, either?"

Her hand was back on his arm, as if he was escorting her down the aisle and not just to her door.

"It's the carriage that turns back into a pumpkin. And I was thinking something along those lines myself, only I had me turning into an ugly stepsister."

Eli stopped and pulled her to him in the middle of her walkway, warning deep and low as his fingertips assured her without hurting her that he wouldn't allow her to do anything but look up at him. "That sounds like a dangerously naughty thought for you to be having, to me."

Had he just called her naughty? And had her butt just begun stinging about five times worse than it had before he'd said that potent word?

"I just thought it; I didn't say it."

Those strong arms found their way around her to pull her against him. "I think you might want to work on a better defense than that, Janey."

She pursed her lips, endeavoring to distract him. "That

from someone who thought Cinderella turned into a pumpkin!"

"Yeah, well," he said, allowing himself to be distracted and guiding her the rest of the way up the walk to the top of her stairs. He took her keys from her, opening the door and peering inside while insisting that she stay on the stoop, only handing them back to her when he had thoroughly inspected the place.

Not wanting to forget her manners as she regarded him, either, she forced herself to look up at him.

"Thank you for having me—"

"I haven't really had you...yet," he teased, a wicked grin on his face as he watched the blush come over her that he knew his words would cause.

Then he reclaimed her again for a kiss that left her leaning weakly against him, which he loved the feel of. Eli pressed his lips to the top of her head and confessed, "If I don't go now, gorgeous, then I never will."

With that, he smacked her smartly on the rump as he turned and headed back to his car. From the driver's side door, practically as he was getting into the car, Eli called to her sternly, "Have a small glass of ginger ale, if you have it, to settle your stomach, then go right to bed, young lady."

Feeling braver than she had with some distance between them, Jane answered back, "Yeah, yeah."

Then he straightened back up, not in the car at all anymore. His very dominant, "Excuse me? Do I need to come in there and make sure you do as I say?" drew a much better response from her.

"No, Eli. I don't have the soda, but I'll go right to bed," Jane answered dutifully.

He gave her a look that made her wonder if she had fresh batteries for her vibrator. "You'd better, little girl. Sleep well."

She wasn't used to anyone being such a caretaker towards her—hell, her mother hadn't been much of one since she was about six. She'd never really gotten much tender loving care from that woman.

Jane was sure that—after all of the very unexpected excitement of the day—she was going to be wired and up all night, despite her sincere intentions to obey him…eventually.

But he turned out to be right. Her head hit the pillow, and she was out like a light.

Chapter 5

JANE HAD BEEN ABSOLUTELY RIGHT, too. She'd been able to live off that day for the next three, and she was still floating several inches above the ground, even though she hadn't heard a word from Eli. That was all right with her. She honestly hadn't expected to. She didn't expect any more from him than what he'd already given her. She could die happy.

And, if he really wanted to see her again, he could have talked to her about that in more detail at any time while they were together that day, or even during the car ride home. But he hadn't, and she was cool with that.

She hadn't cried, she hadn't wailed, she hadn't even binged, which was her usual way of handling sadness or anxious feelings. Well, any feelings, really.

It was better this way, anyway, especially if what she had come to suspect of him was true. She didn't want to think it was, but she hadn't wanted to in college, either, and that fiasco of an experience had left her more than a bit wary of men who looked too good to be true actively pursuing her.

It was near eleven at night, and she was in her pajamas in

bed, deep into plans for a science unit on dolphins, when her phone rang. She was so involved in it—and expecting that it was going to be Sheila calling her at this hour—that she didn't look to see who it was. She just put the phone up to her ear and said, "Hello."

But it certainly wasn't Sheila's voice that answered her. "Why hello, gorgeous!"

If she was ever going to stroke out, it was going to be now. Son of a bitch, he was calling her! *On the phone and everything*, she thought inanely.

Jane did her best to prevail on herself to try to act at least somewhat cool, but even with her suspicions, it was hard to do.

"Oh—Eli. Hi!"

He was sitting in his living room, booted feet propped up on the coffee table—he could do that now that Linds had moved out—and he was distinctly underwhelmed by her greeting. "I hope I'm not waking you up?"

She wanted to continue working while talking to him, but it involved the use of scissors, and she also preferred not to make a high-speed trip to the ER with one or several of her fingers in a plastic baggie, so she put the scissors down as gingerly if they were bombs.

"No, definitely not." So, here was the phone call she'd been craving and dreading in equal measures.

Well, this was going nowhere fast. She sounded distracted or annoyed or something, but he plowed ahead anyway. Any kind of talking to her was preferable to none. "I hope you don't mind me calling you. I got your number from Lindsay."

"No, of course not!" She hoped she didn't sound too mindlessly eager. "And I think I kind of figured the Lindsay part."

Her tone sounded a bit more normal and he relaxed a

bit. "Yeah, she told me to wait three days so that I didn't make you feel like I was stalking you."

That earned him much more of a laugh than he expected.

He thought *she* would feel stalked! That was rich! Jane was rolling, until she realized that he wouldn't have any idea what she was laughing about, and then she forced herself to clear her throat and straighten up.

"Oh. I didn't know about that rule." *Idiot!* Now he's going to think you've not dated much, and he'd be *right*, 'cause you haven't dated *at all!*

At this point—five seconds into this phone call—Jane just put her head in her hand and prayed for a quick death.

"Neither did I! What kind of crap is that? If you're interested in someone, why wouldn't you call them and let them know? See if it's mutual, maybe, and make plans to get together again if it is. Simple. Straightforward. I like things cut and dried. I cannot stand those kinds of games."

"I think I got that about you." Hopefully she did, anyway. Doubts about his motives had begun to swirl around in her head, and this phone call wasn't helping.

"Good. So." Eli swallowed hard. Asking Jane out at this moment, some twenty years later, was even worse than the first time he'd ever done that, in the fifth grade, when he'd asked Amy Bell to go to the movies with him.

She'd said no.

He'd shrugged and gone on to the next girl he liked and asked her the same thing.

But if Jane said no, he didn't know what he'd do. And learning what he had from his sister about her hadn't helped him in the least—in fact, it had made the situation considerably worse.

In general, women had come easily to him, but not until he'd hit high school. Even then, though, he hadn't been a player, although he could have been. Having a sister—and a strong mother—civilized him more than a lot of guys, even some them his friends. He'd dated one girl for pretty much the whole four years, Lia D'Angelo, and they'd broken up when she decided she wanted to go away to college. Not because she'd gone away—he had been quite determined that they could stay together despite that. But she'd gone away and wanted to play around, and he couldn't—and wouldn't—tolerate that.

Since then, he hadn't allowed himself to become quite so involved with one woman. He'd had his share of female companionship in college and afterward. But there hadn't been anyone with whom he'd really clicked, at least not in the pretty specific ways he wanted to.

Sex, he could get any time, and frankly, he did. But he wanted what his parents had—a distinctly old fashioned, loving, committed marriage—and he felt as if he was living in the completely wrong era for that. Especially considering that he intended to discipline his wife, if he saw fit, and not all women were into that kind of thing, especially not as one of the tenets of a committed relationship.

Then he remembered that he'd planned out how he wanted to ask her for himself, for just this reason, putting his own spin on the results of the very revealing conversation he'd had with his sister. "Lindsay and Jake are going to try that new Italian place down in Chittenden Square this Friday. They've heard really good things about it, and they asked if I wanted to go with them. But I don't really want to go alone—would you like to come, as my date?"

In reality, he'd called and asked Lindsay and Jake if they'd come to dinner with him the night after the barbecue, knowing that she and Jane were already well acquainted, if not actually friends. Lindsay, of course, had found that to be a riot, especially when he'd gone so far as to offer to pay for them, too.

"Oh, really, Mr. Big Spender? Wow—millenniums having been reached comes to mind! Does that place have steak? Or lobster? Let's go to a steak or seafood place and really get our money's worth."

He could hear his brother-in-law in the background, firmly warning Lindsay to back off in a no-nonsense tone, and it sounded a lot like the way he had talked to Jane at times on Saturday.

Jake kept Lindsay on a shorter leash than he had—he was much less indulgent than Eli had been, but then he hadn't had to tell her that their parents were gone when she was in middle school, either. But that was probably very good for her. Hell, he knew for a fact that it was extremely good for her. She'd gotten to be a bit bratty, but Jake had made it clear to Lindsay that he wasn't going to put up with that kind of behavior, and he didn't. Eli knew that Lindsay found sitting to be very uncomfortable at times, but he truly thought she was a better—and undoubtedly a happier—person for it.

He had no doubts that Jake adored Lindsay—none at all, from the start—or he would never have been able to sanction their relationship, which he knew was very important to his little sister.

"No, we're going to The Roma. Nowhere else."

Lindsay had sighed deeply. "You two are no fun at all."

"Tell him of course, we'll go," Jake said. "Now, Lindsay," he prompted when she took quite a bit too long to do so for his liking.

"Of course, we'd love to go!" She'd laid it on thick and sarcastically, and Eli heard the crack of what he knew was a swat to her backside, along with Lindsay's pained yelp that accompanied it. When she spoke again, her tone was normal. "We'll be there. Just let us know when."

"I have to ask her first."

She was amazed to hear him sounding more nervous about that than she ever had before about anything. Lindsay laughed. "Jane Medford would follow you to the ends of the earth, even if you didn't ask her to do so."

"What do you mean?"

He could hear her rolling her eyes at him from several miles away. "Men are so fucking oblivious."

"Lindsay, language."

"Sorry, Jake."

It was so strange to hear her be so conciliatory.

"You aren't now, but you will be."

There was a small, awkward pause before she continued. "Jane has had a crush on you since the day she was born."

"Bull."

Lindsay, having already earned a punishment from her husband, wasn't in the mood to argue with her brother and likely earn a much worse one. "Okay. She doesn't. Just let us know when you want us to be there, and we will. Love you, bro."

"Love you, too, sis."

After he'd asked Jane, after it was out there, hanging in the ether, Eli had held his breath. And then he held it some more. And then more.

The silence from the other end of the phone was nerve wracking.

He took it away from his ear to check if the call been dropped. No, they were still connected.

"Jane? Are you okay? Jane?"

Her answer was very watery, and he knew immediately that she was crying. "Uh, well, no, not really."

Eli sat up straight in his chair, wishing he was there with

her now so he could hold her. "Do you need me to come to you? I can be there in ten minutes."

Ten minutes? Did he have a rocket in his backyard that no one knew about? Still, she didn't doubt him. She knew he'd do his damndest to make it so.

He was standing, patting his pockets for his keys, and then she said something that absolutely stunned him.

"Are y-you...you have to be...just look at you! If you are, just please tell me."

He was confused about what she meant. "Tell you what, honey?"

Jane took a deep breath. "Are you paying attention to me to my face, but laughing at me behind my back?" Her voice was so thin and inhibited by the tears she was so obviously holding back that he could barely understand what she was saying. "It's just that, you've never said really anything to me beyond 'hello' and 'goodbye', and you're so beautiful, and I'm just so not. I can't figure out why you're paying so much attention to me when you could have pretty much any other woman you wanted."

He sank back down into the chair, devastated to hear how she was thinking about him and about herself. "Oh, Jane, no."

She was out and out weeping now, and his chest hurt unbearably at the sound.

But almost as soon as his butt touched the cushion, he was up again and pacing back and forth. "Jane, listen to me. I'm going to Facetime you, okay?"

"No! No—I can't right now. Don't call me. I'm all...I'm not..." She wanted to say that she looked uglier than she usually did, but she already knew better than to say anything more.

Eli stopped, speaking to her slowly and gently, but firmly. "Yes, Jane. If you don't answer my call, I *will* be pounding on your door before you know it. And if I have to, I will break it down."

Christ, he would, too! Jane thought. And that would be a-zillion-times worse.

He didn't give her the chance to say or do anything else, the sound of her weeping softly making him disconnect immediately.

Eli punched the buttons as quickly as he could to get back to her, but it took her much longer than he wanted for her to pick up. So, he texted her.

Jane. If I come over there, you're going to have an entirely different —and I suspect much more valid—reason to cry.

She accepted his call immediately.

"Where are you, baby?"

Oh, God, she wished he'd stop using endearments with her and praising her. She wasn't sure which was worse, especially if all of this sudden attention from him was—as she had come to suspect, with Sheila's admittedly reluctant help —a sham.

"M-my room," she sniffed.

"Good. I want you to hunker down under the covers and then put me where you can see me best."

"J-just a s-sec."

"That's okay, babygirl. Take your time. I'll wait. I'll be right here."

Yeah, he had to be faking it. No man was that patient— at least, not according to her girlfriends' numerous and seem-ingly endless complaints about their significant others, anyway.

Eventually, she could stall him no longer. She'd cleared the stuff off her bed, but she didn't have a mirror in her room, and she knew she looked horrible.

Whatever. It didn't really matter, anyway.

So, she maneuvered the phone until she could see him.

She looked so forlorn and unhappy that he wished he had just gone to her.

"Thank you for doing this. I know it must be very uncomfortable for you. I just wanted to make sure that you were okay, to see you with my own eyes. And I wanted you to be able to look me in the eye when I say that I would *never* do that kind of thing. Not to you, not to anyone. I never have, and I never will."

He paused for a moment, collecting his thoughts, knowing that what he was saying now would determine whether or not he had a shot with her. "I know you have a lot of concerns about your weight, and I realize that I will never really know what you've been through because of it. But I think you're gorgeous. I'm sure that's hard for you to believe, but I fully intend to be around more than long enough to get you to accept that as fact, because it is."

The tears had just begun to abate, and now they were back again because of what he was saying and how openly and honestly he was saying it.

"I wish I was there to dry your tears and hold you, little one."

"I wish you were, too."

He smiled at her, looking amazingly handsome, of course. "Well, the first step towards me being around you more to do just that is you going out with me—and Lindsay and Jake—on Friday night. Do you like Italian food?"

She was fat. Of course, she liked Italian food. But she wisely didn't put it to him that way.

"Uh, yeah—yes, I do."

"Good. So, I'll pick you up at seven Friday night."

Jane sighed audibly into the phone. "You're not going to let this go, are you?"

She wasn't crying, although he could see that her breath was hitching and she was sniffling a bit. She was giving him attitude, instead. Video chatting had distinct advantages—he could see when she was rolling her eyes at him.

Eli had to chuckle. "What could possibly have given you the idea that I could be just a wee bit stubborn?" He imbued the last part of that sentence with a reasonably good Scottish accent.

He sounded so angelic and malleable, but she so knew he wasn't. "Oh, all right. Friday at seven," she agreed.

"Great. Thank you. But could you sound a bit less like I'm going to be dragging you off to the stocks?"

"No," she answered, but she was smiling as she did it.

Eli finally let himself resume his comfortable position in his easy chair. "So, are you okay, honey?"

He asked as if he really cared about her answer and would actually listen to it. "I-I'm fine, yeah."

Eli's chin nearly hit his chest, as if he doubted the veracity of her answer. "Are you sure?"

"Yes!" She peeped at him as her panties were nearly incinerated at the searing hot combination of his tone and that look.

"I'm glad. I'll say goodnight then, and you should probably go to sleep."

"Yes, Eli," she said, entirely too docilely.

He chuckled but still said, "That's what I like to hear. Sleep well, Janey."

"You, too, Eli."

"I'll text you or whatever during the week, just to keep in touch."

"That would be nice."

He liked hearing that, too. "Great. Night, baby."

"Night, Eli."

Chapter 6

THAT DINNER WAS the beginning of everything for her—for them—even more so than the cookout.

He'd been prompt, of course, and so had she, coming out the door just after he rang the bell.

"Wow, you're punctual! I like that in a woman."

Jane tried to blow by him, but he caught her arm and literally bent her back over his, giving her a dramatic kiss like something out of the movies that had her secretly worrying about what her neighbors were going to make of that, to say nothing of whether she would end up on her head.

But of course, she hadn't.

Her world had narrowed down to just the two of them as he traced her lips with his tongue then the edges of her teeth, before exploring further as she couldn't help but melt in his arms.

Then, long before she wanted him to, he tipped her back up with ease.

She was totally discombobulated by that, and she was glad to see that she wasn't the only one. He was standing there, looking at her intently as if he couldn't decide whether to ditch his relatives in favor of staying home with her.

He didn't want to do that to Linds and Jake, so he resolved to behave himself, since it seemed he had to. But he kept her as close to him at all times as he could without drawing attention to them, which he knew she would abhor.

It was a medium sized place, purporting to be family run, and judging by its casual, comfortable atmosphere, it seemed it was. Not knowing whether or not she was in the habit of being on time, he'd had Lindsay and Jake put the reservation in their name, so they were already seated when he and Jane got there.

He kept hold of her hand—even as she tried to withdraw it—and tugged her along with him as he headed for their table, having already helped her off with her coat to hang it up in the small entryway, then pulling out her chair for her when they sat down after Lindsay got up to hug them both.

"Jane, do you know Jake?"

"We've met, but we haven't talked much," he supplied for her, offering his hand to shake.

Jane was glad to see that the conversation flowed quite smoothly, and everyone seemed to make sure that she was included in any inside, family jokes.

"It's a bit of a learning curve with these two." Jake smiled at her. "But it's more than worth it." He kissed the backs of his wife's fingers while she blushed.

The menu, for a place that wasn't huge or a chain, was quite extensive.

"Jane, do you like any of the appetizers?" Eli asked, wanting to order one of everything he saw.

"No, thanks. None for me."

His sister looked appalled at that idea, leaning towards Jane and whispering, "Oh, c'mon! We should get three or four of them—moneybags over there is paying for the whole table!" She inclined her head towards her brother. "I say we bleed him dry while we can—he's a notorious tightwad."

Jake's soft, "Lindsay," had Jane's ears pricking up because it sounded deceptively mild but stern at the same time.

And apparently, she was right, because the other woman sat back down immediately—and was that gingerly, too? Or was she just imagining it?

Eli frowned at his sister, then he smiled brightly down at Jane. "The brat is right—I'm paying. Why don't we each get an appetizer and we'll share them? I want you to order whatever you want."

Jane almost smiled at that. If only that were possible; not that she'd gorge herself, even if given the chance, but she would have loved to have tried the cheesy garlic bread.

"No, thank you," she replied primly.

The waitress appeared then and got their drink orders. Lindsay ordered wine, the men, beers, and Jane had an ice water with lemon.

"Don't drink?" Jake asked in a friendly manner. She'd not had beer at the picnic, but then, lots of people don't like beer.

"Not much, really, no."

"You could have a soda, if you want or—" he offered, trying to be helpful and wanting her to enjoy herself.

Jane was looking a bit lost and overwhelmed. "Eli, she can choose for herself what she wants," Lindsay contributed, trying to be helpful to Jane, and not sarcastically, for a change.

He frowned. "Of course, she can."

When the waitress returned, she took their appetizer orders. The three of them ordered mozzarella sticks, the garlic bread, and an antipasto.

"Do we know what we want for our meals, or do you need another minute?"

Everyone seemed to know what they wanted, and the waitress looked at Jane, first. "I'll have the Caesar salad, please."

Jane refused to look at anyone else at the table, because she could literally feel them looking at her as if she was crazy. Everyone but the waitress was staring at her, and she was waiting for Eli to order.

When she was gone, Eli opened his mouth, and Lindsay knew what he was going to say so gave her brother a look and deliberately pre-empted him, posing a question to Lindsay that was designed to draw her out. "So, are you all ready to start teaching?"

Since the question was in her wheelhouse, Jane became her more animated self, and the talk drifted from there to more generic subjects, like how everyone else's jobs were going. Eli and Jake were both ranchers, so they had a lot to talk about, and Lindsay owned a dress shop in a bigger town, not far away. They indulged in a bit of old fashioned small town gossip—noting who was separating or divorcing of the couples they all knew, and they discussed their favorite TV shows. Everyone was in complete agreement that *Stranger Things* was pretty damned good and had been able to maintain a very high standard of quality for both seasons, whereas *The Handmaid's Tale* had been kind of bogged down in its second season, unfortunately.

The guys were sci-fi fans and loved all of the superhero movies that were coming out through DC and Marvel. Jane allowed that she just liked movies—she saw all types of them, from sci-fi to kids' movies, if they looked like they'd be good.

"Don't tell me you like *Deadpool?*" Lindsay groaned.

"Fuck—uh, hell, yes!"

"Good save," Eli commented under his breath with a grin.

"That wouldn't have saved me," Lindsay piped up in a slightly whiney tone, making Jake grin.

"No, it wouldn't have," he agreed firmly.

Jane had a feeling that there was some kind of undertone between the two that she wasn't quite picking up on, but she ignored it in favor of talking about movies—and theatre— both of which she loved.

"I thought the first was better than the second, but how can you not like him?"

"That's what we've been saying!" the boys chimed in.

"There's a *Downton Abbey* movie in the making, and some-time in December, Saoirse Ronan is playing the title role in a movie about Mary, Queen of Scots."

She said her little speech with incredible excitement, but her audience's eyes had glazed over. Apparently, they weren't into that kind of movie. "Sorry. Lost you all. What can I say, I'm a costume-drama slut?"

The whole table began to laugh at that, and that was when the appetizers appeared. It was an enormous amount of food, and dinner was still on its way. Eli prevailed upon her to try some of anyone's she wanted, but she demurred quietly and sipped on her water.

Except for Jane's apparent weirdness about food, which bothered him a bit, although he tried not to let it show, Eli thought that the dinner was going really well, and he loved having her by his side. It had taken her a bit to relax, but that was fine. She seemed happy, although he knew that the inter-play between the new husband and wife had puzzled her, but he wasn't about to get into it now. Certainly, not so early on in things.

He wished she'd eat something other than half of her small salad, but Lindsay had made him aware of not wanting to push food on her if she didn't want it. As he'd said, himself, she was more than capable of making her own decisions.

When they parted, it was later than usual—they'd hung around and practically closed the place down just chatting. Despite how Lindsay teased him, he paid the bill without so much as letting a moth escape from his wallet, and he'd left the waitress a very generous tip, too, for putting up with them for so long.

Lindsay hugged Jane. Eli was glad to see that she hugged her back, and Jake did, too, although less enthusiastically because he didn't know her and didn't want to make her feel uncomfortable. They went their separate ways to their cars, and even though Jake and Lindsay had gotten there before they did, he pulled out of the parking lot before their car did.

Eli wondered if Linds was getting a bit of a talking to from her husband.

"Thank you for dinner. Did you enjoy it?"

"You're welcome, and yes, I did, but I don't think you did."

Her face fell. "I had a great time! I already like Lindsay, and Jake is wonderful. He reminds me a bit of you."

Eli blushed at her compliment. "Yes, but I don't think you liked the food. You didn't finish your salad."

"My stomach's a bit queasy, and I had more than enough of it, thanks." Yet another lie. But it was better than having them—and everyone else in the restaurant—watching her every bite.

"Oh, I'm sorry. Should we get you something for it on the way home?"

"No, thanks. I'll be okay."

He took her hand and kissed her fingers. "You sure? It's no problem to stop—I'll go in and get whatever you want."

"You're sweet, but no. I'll be okay."

He gave her a skeptical look. "Well, all right."

"He says, grudgingly," she teased with a smile.

And he smiled back at her. "Well, I like to look after you, but you thwart all of my attempts."

"I do not!" she argued. "You've taken care of me more in the past two times I've seen you than my mom did from the time I was about six."

"Jesus, Jane!" He sounded horrified, reaching over to squeeze her leg. "I'm so sorry about that!"

"Don't be. It's in the past."

"I know, baby, but still. I wish things had been better for you." Then he switched gears entirely. "Well, then, you really do need very careful looking after, don't you?"

"Nope," she returned firmly. "Been doing that since I was six."

"What happened when you were six, if you don't mind my asking?" It was the wrong question to ask her—he knew it the moment it was out of his mouth. He felt her withdraw immediately.

She minded, but she told him anyway, staring out the window, deliberately not looking at him. "That's when I started to get fat."

Eli didn't say anything to that, but he did pull some ways down a deserted side street, just to give her an enormous bear hug. And while he was still holding her, with his forehead pressed to hers, he whispered huskily, "I want us to date, Jane," then began to bestow tiny kisses all over her face.

She could feel his beard in places against her skin, and it felt incredible. He felt incredible. The whole situation was utterly unbelievable, and he was asking for it to continue, as if she was a normal sized woman.

"I'd be very proud to be able to say you were mine."

Jane took a deep breath, cringing inwardly at everything he was saying, but at the same time, it was the stuff of her dreams! She wasn't at all sure she could do it, though. She didn't think she was anywhere near strong enough.

What if it didn't work out?

She bent down and kissed his fingers where they held hers, as reverently as if she was worshipping him. When she brought her head up, intending to say something, it evaporated as his hand cupped her cheek and he kissed her for all he was worth.

He had a feeling she was going to say a flat out no, and then that would be that. He wanted to prevent that, in any way he could, and if he had to keep kissing her forever, he would. It certainly wouldn't be any kind of a hardship for him.

Eli couldn't keep his other fingers from trailing down the column of her neck, dragging his callused fingertips down very soft skin, to just above where the first button of her dress lay over her cleavage.

She put her palms on his chest and felt it rise with his indrawn breath, but he knew she wanted him to back off, and he did.

"I can't imagine that you're at all used to hearing this but—"

"Don't say no, Jane," he whispered raggedly.

Jane caught his eyes. "I wasn't going to say no; I was going to say that I need to take a little time to think about it."

He breathed an enormous sigh of relief. "You take as much time as you like, darlin'. But while you're doing so, we're going to date."

She had to laugh at that. He was nothing if not persistent! "Doesn't that kind of defeat the whole purpose of me taking time to think about dating you?"

He grinned wholly irreverently. "It doesn't defeat *my* purpose in the least—I'm not particularly worried about yours at the moment."

His unabashed attitude made her chuckle. "Well, I suppose we could see each other once every other—"

"Day," he supplied eagerly.

"Year," she ended cheekily.

"No."

"Month?" She was negotiating with him, so she knew she'd already lost.

He made the game show buzzer sound. "Nope. Try again."

"Uhhhhhhh, once every two weeks?"

"Sorry. You lost. But I do have some delightful non-parting gifts for you."

It was another of his fantastic kisses—just what she wanted!

When he lifted his head from hers, still occasionally returning to her mouth as if he couldn't get enough of it, she asked, "I take it you want to see me every week, even though I haven't actually agreed to date you?"

He nodded emphatically.

"And the dichotomy there doesn't bother you?"

"Absolutely not, I can assure you," he returned seriously. "When you do agree—and you will—then we'll go out two or three times a week."

She looked surprised.

"Not enough?" He frowned.

Jane had to laugh at his enthusiasm. "No, I'm just amazed that you want to spend any time with me at all, frankly."

"Jane." Her name held a wealth of warning.

But she didn't back down. "I'm sorry, but you should be in movies, and even if I was rail thin, I'd still be wondering what the hell you were doing with me."

"In that case, you'd still be getting spanked, but for thinking in a different way that was incorrect."

Jane grimaced. "Do you have an answer for everything?"

"Yes, ma'am, I do."

"Oh, bloody hell, don't you dare 'ma'am' me. I've been getting 'ma'amed' since I was about eleven."

"I'm sorry. I'll try to remember that, but 'sir' and 'ma'am' are pretty popular around here. Everyone teaches their kids to call adults that."

"I know. Of course, one of the few advantages to being fat and looking older than I was did mean that I could buy cigarettes and liquor long before I was legal to do either."

Still holding onto her, Eli leaned back a bit to look down at her, askance. "You don't smoke or drink—why would you do either of those things?"

Jane shrugged. "Friends wanted both of them."

"Sheila," he pounced. "I knew she was a bad influence."

"No more so than you are, Mr. Ridgeway."

"I'll wear that title proudly." Eli waggled his eyebrows at her outrageously, loving making her laugh.

She knew she was blushing, but there wasn't much she could do about it.

"How about if I live up to it right now?"

Jane gulped hard suddenly, as the rest of her whole body clenched. "N-now?"

Eli reached out and adjusted her, so that she was comfortable, her back to his front. Sighing raggedly as she settled back against him. "Oh, God, yes, now. I won't go too far, I promise, but I just want to touch you again, like I did in my study, only more so. I've been craving the feel of your quivering little kitty in my palm ever since." His hands were traveling slowly down her arms as they still managed to keep her in place, somehow. "Unbutton your dress for me, Jane."

She looked around them furtively, and he noticed.

"This is that never completed residential development off Harrington Ave. There are streetlights to keep the rabble away, but no one to see us. I want you to know that I would never put you in any kind of danger, Jane."

He was very glad when she nodded that she understood that about him, and she even obeyed him and began to do as he asked. "Good girl." Eli squeezed her arm. But she halted just below her breasts. "Did I tell you to stop, sweetheart?"

She wiggled against him—Jesus, he wished she wouldn't do that, but damn, he was glad she did! But she finished the job, if with charming reluctance, and he peeled the sides of her dress far apart, putting her on display in the lamplight.

"My God, woman! Gorgeous doesn't even begin to touch you, but I'm going to!"

"Eli, stop! You have to stop saying things l-like th-that." Her protest ended on a long, stuttering sigh as his fingers delved into her bra and easily located her nipples, pinching them lightly until they were hard and achy.

"What were you saying that I have to do, Jane?" he asked, as if daring her to come up with a coherent response while he continued to brush his fingertips over the barest tips of her nipples then capturing them to pinch them a bit hard in contrast.

She drew a breath to reply to him, but all that came out was a long groan.

"That's what I like to hear!" He was kissing her neck at the same time, and apparently, that was a considerable erogenous zone for her, because it was driving her crazy!

"You came so quickly the last time. Is that usual for you?"

Jane was even less able to answer him now than she was before. She kept opening her mouth, but all that came out was a lot of panting.

Eli chuckled warmly, understanding exactly where she was. "Doesn't matter in the least. Forget I asked. Just concentrate on where I'm touching you and nothing else, hear?"

She nodded languidly, encouraging his endeavors by arching herself against him.

"Open your legs a bit, baby. I want to touch there, most of all."

Jane was gone but not quite that far. He'd have to reach all the way down over her rolls of fat to get to her, and she wasn't at all sure she was comfortable with him doing that, and she stiffened.

But he was prepared for her to balk at his instructions. Perhaps if she was worrying about avoiding a punishment, Eli thought, she wouldn't be so concerned about her body. "Do as I said, Jane, or do I have to tan your hide before you'll obey me?"

That got him a whimper that nearly had him jizzing behind his zipper.

"But, Eli—" She sounded anxious and was still tense in his arms.

"No, Jane." Firm and unyielding. "Obedience or punishment. That's your choice, every time I ask you to do something."

She gave him a surprisingly petulant groan, then she moved her thighs apart.

"Good girl. That's always the right choice."

She was quite amply rewarded, seconds later, feeling the fingers of his right-hand brushing against that triangle of sparse, light hair, then reaching down past it to find what they really wanted.

"Oh, my, babygirl, you are so buttery!" He sounded downright awestruck.

Jane had never heard it called that, but she liked it.

"That's wonderful!" He moved his fingers upward, saying, when he found her clit, "And what have we here, hmm? I think this little bud is crying out for some attention."

He took his time, trying to remember what she'd liked

from before, swirling and brushing and tapping and stroking her, committing to his considerable mind every sigh, every mewl, and definitely every moan.

Long before he was done, she was clutching at the arm that lay against her for dear life.

"Eli, please!"

"Oh, I do like to hear you beg me, Janey. Do it again for me." His chin was atop her head, and she was putty in his hands.

It was much harder to do the second time, when she was thinking about it and thinking about the fact that he had told her to do it.

But he had slowed his delicious movements almost to a stop, and she couldn't have that! She'd die if he stopped! "Please, Eli!"

"That's better."

He watched her—everything about her, especially about this intimate side of her—as he brought her closer and closer to her release, wanting to learn everything he could about how to best bring her to pleasure.

And as he slowly drove her over the edge in a wild, crazy frenzy that he didn't think she even realized was happening to her, he moved himself against her bottom, and even from behind his zipper, he managed to find his own release.

After holding her for a good long while, cleaning them both up and then just keeping her safely embraced while she drifted back to earth, he forced himself to put her back in her seat, buckled her seatbelt and dropped her off at her house a few minutes later, after being endearingly kind and solicitous to her on top of everything else and renewing her feelings of deep guilt.

"Is your stomach still iffy?" he asked as they walked to her door.

She crossed her fingers where he couldn't see. "A little."

"How about if I go get you some ginger ale? You didn't have it last time, and I bet you haven't had a chance to buy any."

"No, I don't want to put you out, and I promise you, I'll be fine."

He looked doubtful. "Are you sure?"

She laughed. "Yes, I'm sure."

"Well, then, I'll be on my way."

"Text me when you get home, please!" She hoped that wasn't being too demanding or forward, but she liked to know that he was okay, too.

"Of course! I have to say good night to you and tuck you in, anyway."

When he had driven away, Jane closed the door and leaned back against it, still deep in bliss and contracting occasionally, but she didn't stay there for long.

She was starving!

Jane rummaged through her snack cupboard and came up with a party sized bag of Lay's potato chips—the plain kind. Old school. She liked them with dip or without, only right now, she couldn't be bothered to see if she had any dip that hadn't become a science experiment in the back of her fridge.

It was a surprisingly short amount of time before there was a knock at her door; they were much quicker than usual, not that she was complaining.

So, still clutching her bag of chips, one actually hanging out of her mouth, she opened the door and pushed open the screen door, using her foot to keep it open, not really paying attention to who it was.

She thought she knew.

But while she was otherwise occupied, she heard a man's very deep, very unhappy sounding voice. "Jane Medford, you are soon going to be in a *world* of hurt."

Fuck.

Fuck. Fuck. Fuck. Fuck.

Fuckety-fuck fuck fuck.

Her face fell and her complexion paled by several shades.

Jane had miscalculated badly. How was she supposed to know that he would get all chivalrous and come back to give her a bottle of ginger ale, which was the first thing he put on the little hall tree, in front of her, in the same bowl with her money, as he stepped into her tiny entryway.

Then he proceeded to pluck the bag of chips from her hand and put those down there, too, before taking several steps into her house. She had the errant thought that it had been a while since she'd vacuumed, but he didn't look around at all. He never took his eyes off of her. Instead, he crossed his arms over his chest and stood there, staring at her.

Jane, meanwhile, had mirrored his steps forward with steps backward of her own, as she was busily trying to finish the handful of chips she'd had in her mouth when all hell had broken loose. But he hadn't allowed her to maintain any of the distance she was trying to put between them, proceeding to back her up against the far wall of her living room, by the kitchen, and keeping her there with nothing but the force of his presence and his personality.

That was quite enough for her.

And she was terribly afraid, as she stood there before him like a naughty schoolgirl before the principal, feeling smaller than she ever had in her life, that all hell was going to break loose again in just a few minutes, and it wasn't going to make him any happier than he was now.

In fact, it was going to make him unhappier. A lot unhappier.

"What do you have to say for yourself, Jane?"

The disappointment that was blatant in his tone was

horrendous, but her mind couldn't help noting that he had just the perfect voice and tone for a Dom.

She shrugged. "What *can* I say?"

"Was your stomach ever upset?"

What could it hurt to tell him the truth now? "I was really anxious about the dinner, and I don't eat much when I'm that nervous, but, no, my stomach wasn't upset," she finally admitted, wondering if she'd just seen headlights from a car turning into her driveway.

Crap, crap, crap!

She was feeling even more nervous now, literally shifting back and forth on her feet as he questioned her, nearly yelping when she heard the sound of a car door closing, although he hadn't seemed to have heard it.

He seemed oblivious to everything but her. Surprisingly, he didn't sound like he was pissed, although he had to be.

And if he wasn't now, he was going to be in a few seconds.

There was a knock on the door that made Jane cringe, and he swiveled to look back at it, then back at her, one eyebrow up. "You're expecting company at this hour?"

Jane bit her lip, twisting her fingers in front of her, wishing she'd just faint and get it over with already. "Well, not exactly."

Eli was already at the door, pulling it open. Then, when he saw who it was, he turned to give her an incredulous look. Then he turned back to the kid on the stoop.

"Dominoes' delivery?"

For a good long while, they—all three of them—stood there, not moving or saying anything.

Then the guy said, understandably, "Should I take it back?

Jane made as if to get him money for the pie, but she stopped in her tracks at the look Eli gave her. "You, stay," he commanded sternly. She moved back so she could lean against the wall and worry her lip.

"No, we'll take it," Eli told the young kid. He then paid him for it, with a big tip, closing the door firmly before he executed an about face and pinned her with his gaze, pizza in hand. "I'm quite sure at least one of us will have worked up an appetite later, although the other of us isn't going to be sitting very comfortably while she eats it."

Chapter 7

ELI PUT the pizza on the counter in her kitchen then came back to where she was, asking shrewdly, "Did you have a stomach ache at the barbecue? And I would suggest that you don't lie to me and make things exponentially worse for yourself."

Jane shook her head.

"No, say it to me while you look me in the eye, Jane."

That was a horrible thing for anyone with a conscience to have to do, but she did it. "I didn't have a stomach ache at the barbecue."

He knew there was a lot more to it than just her lying to him. From what he'd gleaned about her from his sister, she wasn't known to be a liar, and he was predisposed to think that this was wrapped up in things that had been torturing her from within for a long time.

But that didn't excuse her behavior as far as he was concerned.

He crossed his arms over his chest. "Do you know why I find myself very unhappy with you at the moment?"

Jane dissolved into tears. "Yes, but please understand that I'm not any happier with myself, either."

A muscle jumped in his jaw. "I might not know you that well yet, but I think I get that. Still, a lie is a lie, and you've told me two, already. Is there any other naughtiness you've been up to that I should know about? Better tell me now, little girl. If I find out later that you've not come clean now, while you can, it'll go that much harder on you."

He didn't expect her to, but she nodded her head up and down.

"More lies?"

She began to cry harder. "Kind of."

Eli didn't hold with "kind of" lying, either. "Tell me what they are, now, please."

Somehow, Eli's civility made it even worse for her. But she met his eyes and said, tears streaming down her cheeks, "When we were at the barbecue, you asked me to dance, and I said I didn't dance. That's not exactly right."

"How so? Explain."

"I can dance, I just won't when there's anyone else around."

He seemed surprised to hear that. "And?"

"I-I don't know if it counts, but I told you that I didn't bring my bathing suit."

"Yes."

"Well, I didn't bring one because I don't own one—haven't in decades. The idea of going to buy one—" She shook her head. "I'd sooner die. I know how to swim, but I don't do it."

He nodded, then surprised her by hauling her into his arms and holding her very tightly. "Thank you for telling me that—all of it. You're very brave." Eli took a step back and brushed the side of his thumbs against her cheeks. "You're also very naughty, and I am going to blister that behind of yours."

Then he turned her around and smacked her bottom. "I assume your bedroom is down the hall?"

"Yes."

"Go change."

"Into what?"

"Your bathrobe. Nothing more than that, Jane," he cautioned, "or I'll keep you completely naked through the whole punishment."

Now, that was a terrifying thought!

She had a big, fluffy, sea foam green robe with a belt that she loved, and although she was very apprehensive, she forced herself to go out of her room to stand near him in the living room wearing just that.

She wasn't sure exactly what he was doing, but when he turned back, he was sniffing the very fingers that had brought her off not long ago, and her breath caught in her throat.

"I was deep breathing these on my way home when I decided to bring you the ginger ale I thought you needed."

Jane looked suitably ashamed—she hoped.

Eli sank down on her couch and patted his thigh.

Jane came to him as slowly as she thought she could get away with and went to position herself over his lap.

He chuckled softly. "I like the way you're thinking, and you're going to end up there in a minute. But I want to hold you for a moment and talk to you, first."

That was fine with her! When he'd held her after he'd spanked her at the cookout, it was one of the safest, most cared about she'd ever felt in her life. So, it didn't take any coaxing, really, for her to curl herself up on his lap.

And he was a big enough man that she fit, too!

After drawing a deep breath, Eli began to speak. "I know

there are a lot of things underlying why you acted as you did, babygirl, and we're going to talk more about them after your punishment." He felt her grow instantly rigid at his words, but he didn't let that stop him. "And I can't pretend to understand what you've gone through. But the bottom line for me—and for you," he pointed out by patting it, "is that you lied to me—multiple times. I'll give you the benefit of the doubt—because from what I know of you, you're a good person—that you didn't want to, but you felt you had to in all of those situations."

He caught her chin with his fingers and made Jane look at him. "But that is not how this is going to go between us. I will do my utmost to try to understand how you've learned you have to approach things in your life. I'll bend over backwards to make any accommodation I can to make things easier for you and maybe help you feel better about yourself along the way. But I will *not* be lied to, Jane. I just won't. I think I've said something like that to you already, although it didn't stop you."

She was weeping, and he wiped as many of the tears away that he could.

"You're going to get a bit—just a bit, mind you—of a Mulligan, though, because we're so new, and you don't know me very well, either. You don't know that I demand honesty of you because I will give it to you, unfailingly. You can trust me and tell me things like that, and I know that learning to do so will take time and patience on my part—that I'll have to show and not just tell you—that I'm worthy of your trust, and I will."

As he spoke, he turned her over so that she was in the position she'd originally tried to get into, and he'd arranged the bottom of her robe up around her waist, revealing what he'd already suspected to be the perfect spankable bottom.

And that was exactly what he proceeded to do. He didn't

lecture—although he usually would—because she already knew why she was there. Her skin there was very fair, never having felt the kiss of the sun, he'd bet. He'd very much like to change that for her.

And he was certainly going to change the color of it now!

Jane could only imagine how ungainly she looked at the beginning of the spanking as she tried to avoid the swats he was delivering with a hundred percent accuracy, regardless of her efforts. But the longer it went on, the less she worried about things like that—the less she was capable of doing so, because she was too preoccupied with how her backside was being singed! Without the slightest concern about what a spectacle she was making of herself, she bucked and writhed and kicked her legs, but he held her still for each and every smack.

She didn't even notice when she started crying—all of a sudden, she just was, and there was a damp spot on the couch beneath her head to prove that she'd been doing it for a while.

She'd thought it was over when he stopped smacking her with agonizing regularity and strength, but when she went to get off his lap, he stopped her.

"Where do you think you're going, missy?"

"Y-you're not d-done?" she sniffed loudly, beyond caring that her face was red and her hair was stuck to her damp cheeks.

"No, I'm not. I'll let you know when you can get up, but until then, you should assume that this is where I want you."

Her loved the sound of her meek, "Yes, Eli."

His next question startled—and alarmed—her.

"You have a hairbrush?"

She gulped through tears. "Yes."

"Wooden, I wonder?"

Son of a bitch! It was one of the few nice things she'd

inherited from her grandmother! Made of mahogany, with beautiful roses painted on the back, it was heavy and solid as fuck!

Her long pause—coupled with all of the fidgeting she was doing when he wasn't even spanking her—made him suspect he was onto something. "Jane."

Suddenly, she seemed to relax over him as she finally responded, "Yes, but—"

Seconds later, he was helping her up.

"Go get it for me, please," he commanded in a no-nonsense tone.

Jane gave him a pitiful gaze. "No, Eli, please!"

His eyebrows rose nearly to his hairline. "Yes, Jane. Be happy I'm not taking off my belt. Hurry now, or I will."

That sent her scurrying to bring it back to him from her bedroom, and she was back over his lap again much too quickly for her comfort.

She felt him hefting the brush and knew he was inspecting it before he brought it down on her butt. "Very nice. They definitely made them dual purpose back then."

Jane squealed in protest at that, but she soon was squealing for a very different reason. And she continued to squeal and groan and, finally, on the last furious volley of tremendous smacks, emitted a small but unmistakable scream with each one of them.

Through it all, he'd held her fast with an arm around her waist, and he had never lost his control of her. Eli expected that she'd do her best to avoid what she could of her punishment, but he didn't allow her attempts to interfere in any way. When, at the end, her legs had kicked up a bit further than he preferred, he had simply put one of his own over them—noting how that increased both her sobs and her signs of impotent frustration.

Frankly, he hated to end it. He could spank her forever—

although there were certainly a lot of other things he'd like to do to her, too.

So, he stopped but, again, kept her there, over his lap for long moments while he spoke to her in a soothing tone. "It's okay now, Jane. It's all over, all wiped away. No more guilt, and no recriminations or anything like that from my end. Your punishment has earned you complete forgiveness from me, and I hope you can feel it in your heart. I also hope you can fully forgive yourself, too, although I think you probably hold onto guilt when you don't need to, but we'll work on that together. I think frequent spankings will help you with that, help you to let go of those kinds of feelings."

She certainly liked the sound of that—except, of course, the spanking part.

He helped her up then followed her, reaching down to lift her into his arms and carry her into her bedroom.

Jane had never expected him to be in her tiny room, but he dwarfed it, looking terribly out of place amongst the lace and frill and ruffles she'd indulged herself in when she'd redecorated the place.

But he didn't seem to notice as he lay her down on the bed, on her back. Jane tried to scramble onto her side to relieve some of the stinging that had gotten worse in that position, but Eli, who had moved to the end of the bed, had caught hold of her ankle, forcing her to turn onto her back.

"No, Jane, there's going to be no escaping the pain of that bottom for a while, I'm afraid." He didn't sound very sorry about that, and she doubted he was. "But I think you'll find that it adds something to what's going to happen next."

As he spoke, he was divesting himself of his clothes. His suit coat was already gone, and he didn't even bother to unbutton his shirt, instead, popping all the buttons in one savage movement, as if he couldn't bear it touching him any longer. His chest was a magnificent sight, and Jane's mouth went Sahara dry as she stared at it.

Then he unbuckled his belt, snicking it out of the loops and holding it, doubled over for a moment as he looked from it to her then back again, but then he dropped it on the floor. His pants were next, until he was standing there in just his underwear.

And then, nothing.

Christ, he was a sinfully gorgeous man! She shouldn't be doing this with him—she was a troll in comparison! He was Prince Charming to her Medusa!

But he didn't know what was going on in her head—or he suspected but was ignoring her, was more likely. He'd already put his knee on the end of the bed, crawling up with his hand out, with which he caught the hem of her robe—which was mostly off her, anyway—pulling it out from under her as deftly as a magician pulling a table cloth out from under china and throwing it behind him while he descended eagerly.

He is Jason Momoa to my Wicked Witch of the West, her mind screamed.

Eli fell greedily upon her, mouth open, tongue already licking here and there, making her jump as he moved further up the bed—further up her.

As he lay atop the legs she was holding primly together, his mouth closed around an erect nipple, and her mind abandoned her entirely at the feeling of him suckling so strongly.

"Open your legs for me, Jane," he crooned huskily, although she knew it wasn't a request. As he looked directly into her eyes, his fingers replaced his mouth, and he worried those raspberry tips mercilessly—tapping them, pinching them, twisting them—and watching her closely—too closely —as she reacted to each type of touch.

Jane licked her lips, which had become parched from

panting, knowing he expected her to obey him, but not at all certain that she could.

As suddenly as if she weighed nothing, she was flipped over onto her tummy and given five vicious smacks on her already terribly sore behind, then flipped back.

Those movements had set her to crying again, but it had also left him some of the way between her legs.

When she looked up at him through her tears, he had an expectant look on his face. "I can keep this up for a lot longer than I think you'll want me to, honey."

Slowly, with severe reluctance that he tried to kiss away with only a small amount of success, Jane eventually complied and felt his weight pressing against where she most wanted him to be.

Well, most of her wanted him to be, anyway.

Her mind was still whispering loudly that he shouldn't want to do this with her, but there was tangible evidence to the contrary pressing against her upper thigh at the moment.

"Perfect," he complimented, kissing her deeply, then proceeding to lick and lave his way down the center line of her body, his soft beard tickling her here and there as he held her legs a bit wider apart than she had originally offered him, making more room for himself between them.

Jane jumped when the first thing he did when he arrived at the spot he'd been aiming for was to lean forward and press his entire face into it, his nose parting her lips, facial hairs deliciously soft against her. She could feel him getting her wetness on him and tried to pull back, but he'd already looped his arms around her thighs and she couldn't move.

When he looked up at her, she could see the damp spots of herself on his face and in his beard that he wasn't bothering to wipe away. "I have been anointed," he breathed roughly, "and I want *more*."

And he took more, tugging her even closer to him,

forcing her legs a bit further back, and settling his mouth greedily over her lady parts.

It was a maelstrom of sensuality for Jane, who had never experienced anything like this before—but she didn't think anything could have really prepared her for it in any way. She was so attuned to him, too sensitive to everything he did, that she found herself moaning so constantly that she became self-conscious about it and began to try to fight the urge.

Eli's head came up very quickly once she did. "Did I do something you don't like?"

"Fuck no!" she sighed, and he had to grin.

"Then why have you gone all quiet on me, lovely?"

Her entire body flushed hotter than it already was at that question and its endearment.

"Well, I, uh, thought I was begin, uh, too loud," she confessed in a barely-there whisper.

His smile just broadened at that. "No such thing, little girl. Be as loud as you like! When I hear you moan, your mouth might as well be wrapped around my cock. I swear, sometimes, I'm definitely going to come just from making you come!"

And then he proceeded to not give her much of a choice about how loud she was, because she lost all ability to curb the lewd and lascivious sounds she was making, and that did seem to drive him on.

It wasn't much after that that she climaxed beneath the ministrations of his lips and tongue, reaching down to grasp at his broad shoulders as something solid to hold onto as her world spun out on a wave of ecstasy that he deliberately drew out as long as he could, before allowing her to collapse, fully sated.

"I'm not complaining, you understand," he said as he kissed his way wetly back up her body, "but you come really quickly! I think I'll take it as a compliment. But I intend to get to know you well enough to draw it out for you more."

"You're—" She drew in a panting breath. "Going." Another breath. "To kill me." More panting. "If you do that!"

"Oh, no, there are great delights in delayed gratification!" His long length was stretched out over her, his stiff, aching cock lying between her lips. "And I intend to have all of you, Jane. No more 'will we date or won't we'. We're dating. Exclusively, from this moment on."

He looked down at her expectantly, as if he thought she was going to object.

At that moment, he could have told her pretty much anything and she would have agreed.

"Yes, Eli."

He nodded emphatically. "Damn straight!"

He wanted to take more time with her, show her just how much he adored every inch of her body, even though she'd already orgasmed, but he knew he was nearly at the end of his rope.

So, Eli leaned back a bit, reaching his hand down between them to set the seeping head against her equally sopping entrance.

"Look at me, Jane. Sweetheart," he whispered as he began to press into her.

She did as she was told, but he wasn't getting very far, for some reason, and Jane was looking downright pained, the more he tried.

Then it struck him.

"Jane, you've done this before, haven't you?" he asked incredulously.

There were tears in her eyes and she was biting her lip as she shook her head slowly back and forth.

"You're a virgin."

A short, sharp nod, then she closed her eyes, not wanting to see if she'd made him angry.

A big hand came up to cup her cheek. "Jane, honey, I wish I had thought to ask you about that. I just assumed, and I shouldn't have. Can you forgive me?"

Her eyes came open wide at his words. He was taking the blame all on himself.

"Of—of course! There's nothing to forgive!" she said, and she meant it.

Eli was downright disgusted with himself, and he looked and sounded it. "Of course, there is! If I'd been smart enough to question you about it, I would have done some things differently."

Jane looked up into his eyes and said very clearly, "I wouldn't want you to have done anything differently. Nothing at all."

He blushed at that and leaned down to kiss her, long and slow. When he levered himself up a bit, he vowed, "I'm not trying to brag or anything, but I'm concerned about my size. But I'll go as slowly and carefully as I can."

"Eli, I'll be fine."

He found it strange that she should be reassuring him about such things, but she was right. He proceeded with as much care for her as he could muster when his cock desperately wanted him to plunge heavily into her. And when she had accepted him fully, he asked anxiously, "Are you okay?"

It was snug; there was no denying it. She was being stretched much further than any gynecologist had ever opened her, and it did hurt a little.

But it was also excruciatingly pleasurable! Almost unbearably so!

He looked so concerned about her that Jane wrapped her arms around him and kissed him. "I don't want you to worry about me. If I'm uncomfortable, I'll let you know. But if it keeps feeling like it does now, I'm going to come again before you do!"

"Damn," he growled at her. "The idea of you coming around my cock, tightening and clenching at me—Jesus, woman!"

He hadn't lasted very long, either, reaching down at the end to grasp her still hot cheeks and squeezing them until she squeaked. It was the only real sign of discomfort she'd shown him, for which he was very grateful.

Eli held her in his arms for a long time afterward, utterly unwilling to let her go. He talked to her, too, about some of the things he'd said he would before he'd made love to her, and although he felt her tense when he began, he kept touching and stroking her and speaking in a calm, soothing tone, which seemed to relax her somewhat.

"I want to say something to you that I know you won't believe. Nobody sitting down to dinner with you cares how much you eat. And, if anyone—whether you're sitting with them or not—ever makes you think that they do, they'll have to deal with *me*," he threatened protectively.

Jane smiled up at him, but he could tell she didn't trust what he was saying in the least. That was okay. He'd prove it to her, one way or the other.

Although he knew he was risking upsetting her, he asked, "What you thought I was doing to you—acting as if I was interested in you only to laugh at you—did some guy actually do that to you?" Eli didn't give her a chance to answer him before he added menacingly, "And, if someone did, do you, by any chance, know where he's living now so I can beat the crap out of him, please?"

She could feel his fists clenching as he held her, before he forced them to relax. Jane took a long moment to answer, and she cried a bit when she finally got the nerve to. "Yes, someone did. But that was a long time ago."

Another growl from him, but for a very different reason.

"And you don't have to beat him up. He was just an asshole I'll never see again."

"I would enjoy it enormously, though." He sounded wounded that she wouldn't let him.

"I take it you didn't have a crush on him like you do on me?"

She went still next to him, and he wondered, too late, if that wasn't a very smart thing to say.

Jane began to fight, tooth and nail, to get away from him. Forget what Danny Zullo had done to her during her sophomore year in college. He'd just devastated her with one offhand question! Jane didn't think she'd ever in her life been so deeply embarrassed and humiliated.

And the cause of that shame and degradation was staunchly refusing to let her go.

He began to apologize to her, saying he was sorry repeatedly, until it became like a chant as he was forced to subdue her completely.

Later, Jane would have to seriously consider just how easily it was that he had done that, but not now. Now she wanted to be anywhere he wasn't!

Using that hypnotically calming tone of his, he continued to apologize, but occasionally threw in a "Jane" or "babygirl" as he methodically caught her flailing arms above her head and simply lay himself atop her, his legs forcibly encroaching between hers.

When she continued to resist him, his face set and he took her, in one powerful stroke, until he could feel that he had claimed as much of her as he could.

Jane screamed, slamming her hips up against his when he would have pulled out because he thought he'd hurt her.

But then he chuckled evilly as she whimpered in a needy

tone, and said, "Someone likes being restrained, doesn't she? You can bet I won't forget that, Jane."

Then he proceeded to wipe her mind of any thoughts but his cock, his mouth, and his fingers on her clit, pumping into her, snapping himself into her, changing up the rhythm when she sounded close, and making her wait until she was begging him to let her come.

"All right, baby. But no more trying to get away from me."

The room rang with the sounds of her screams as he set her on a course of orgasms that he kept up until his own harsh cry joined hers and he spilled himself into her depths.

Wiped, he lay on top of her when he knew he should get up and see to her, but he didn't think he could move.

She was pulling at her wrists, and he opened his eyes to find her trying to escape. He forced himself back to full consciousness but didn't move and didn't release her. "I'm not going to let you go until you listen to me about your crush."

Jane looked stricken at that edict, but he was unyielding.

"I'm very flattered that you had a crush on me, probably because I had one on you, too."

"You did not!" she yelled.

One eyebrow up. "Are you calling me a liar, Jane?"

She pursed her lips together. "Nooo!"

"I should hope not. I always saw you around town and at the cookout, but you were so obviously trying not to be seen by me—by anyone—that I didn't think I could really approach you without scaring the crap out of you and sending you running. I didn't have the time that I would have wanted to devote to you, anyway, so I just…let you go, always keeping an ear out for gossip about town as to whether or not you were seeing someone."

"Bullshit," she spat out.

Eli shrugged. "It's the truth, whether or not you believe it.

Regardless, there is nothing for you to be embarrassed about in having a crush. I'm humbled and honored by it."

"Piled high and deeper," she spat again.

"Do I need to impress on you that I don't lie, Jane?" His hand found a sore cheek. She tried to cringe away, but there was nowhere to go but into him.

"No."

He knew she wasn't happy, but he wanted to get past that subject. That pizza had been calling to him for the past few minutes, and he intended to get some!

Eli surprised her by jumping up then, hitting the bathroom, then heading for the kitchen. "Do you have a pizza stone?"

Jane was busy wallowing in self-pity on her bed.

"On top of the fridge," she informed him in a forlorn tone.

Eli popped the pizza into the oven and returned to find her looking pouty. It was an adorable look on her.

So, he decided to give her something else to be preoccupied about, holding her chin up and her eyes on his as he asked her, "How many pieces of pizza do you usually eat? And I'm quite sure I won't have to remind you for a while not to lie to me."

That did the trick.

Her face was perpetually bright red around him, and she didn't think that was likely to change anytime soon.

"But it does depend, though."

He gave her a clearly doubtful look. "On what, pray tell?"

"How much else I've had to eat before I get to the pizza —and it also has to do with the size of the slices, of course. A thin crust piece being much smaller than a slice of pan." She peeped up at him. "TMI?"

"No, it was very well thought out and informative.

However, what I want to know now is how many slices do you want? And 'none' is not a choice. Neither is 'one'."

Jane bit her lip. "Uh, three?" But she really wanted four. "No, four." She forced herself to look up at him and say it. "Four. I'm starving!"

Her reward for being truthful was a quick kiss. "Good girl! A woman after my own heart! You should have ordered two!" he said as he headed back towards her kitchen.

"I didn't know I was having company at the time," she shot back in a disparaging tone.

He didn't say anything to that, so she wandered out in the robe she found crumpled on the floor of the bedroom to watch him make his way around her kitchen rather well. Damn, he was a fine-looking man!

She mentioned that she was kind of surprised at his comfort level in the kitchen.

As he discovered plates, napkins, hot mitts and a spatula, he said, "Who do you think cooked for Lindsay after my parents were gone?"

Jane's hand covered her mouth. How could she have been such a jerk? "Oh, Eli, I'm sorry!"

He turned and flashed her a devastating smile. "Don't be, baby. I loved them, they loved me—and Linds—and they gave me an excellent model of what I want in a committed relationship."

Over pizza shared in the middle of her too small bed, so that they were constantly touching each other every time they moved, laughing and learning to tease each other, talking and making love and then doing it all over again, they bonded very tightly to each other that night, a bond that only strengthened over the next weeks and months of seeing each other as often as they could possibly manage.

Or at least, that was what Jane had thought, anyway.

Chapter 8

IT WAS A WHIRLWIND ALMOST YEAR. Everything about her life had seemed utterly perfect—her job was great—her first year of teaching went wonderfully, her friends were terrific, and being Eli's girlfriend was indescribably phenomenal!

He was everything she'd always dreamt he would be, and so many things she never thought of. She had never felt like she was the center of someone's world before, but he definitely made her feel that way. Emails and texts were always waiting for her in the morning, and he'd always check in during the day, even if it was just to send her a stupid meme he'd found or to say his day was going crappy, but that he knew that it would get better once they were together.

They began spending most of their time at his place, only because it was bigger, and he had a king-sized bed that Jane had immediately fallen in love with, and they had given every inch of it—and then some—a workout.

Even after they'd parted, if they did, he insisted that she let him know when she got home, and then he tucked her in. Sometimes, when he was traveling, especially, they both left

Facetime up all night. He liked to be able to check on her throughout the night, and she liked the sound of him snoring. Eli had confessed to her that others had found it annoying, but she found it very comforting, for some reason.

Except for those occasional trips, he took her everywhere with him. Cattleman's Association meetings, business dinners, and they saw Linds and Jake on the regular, too. Lindsay seemed to be genuinely happy at her brother's happiness, and she immediately began treating Jane like a sister.

The two men were both glad their women got along so well, although they were each a bit concerned that—together —they might get themselves into a heap of trouble. Lindsay and Jane had pretended innocence of that possibility, of course, but when they were alone, they allowed that that judgment probably wasn't too far off.

Although they both must've known what the other had signed up for in those two men, they hadn't really broached that delicate subject between themselves yet. They did offer each other sympathetic looks when one was sitting gingerly across the table from the other—and occasionally exchanged them when they both were sitting on hot seats!

And Eli—like Jake—didn't show any kind of restraint or embarrassment about telling her to behave in front of the other couple, either, but she certainly did.

Luckily, Lindsay had come to the rescue, the first time Eli had said "Jane" to her in *that* tone, and she couldn't help but turn beet red. She'd leaned forward and cupped her hand next to her mouth to whisper, not so quietly, "No worries. Mine's a bossy a-f so-and-so, too."

Jane's eyes went wide at that. She thought Lindsay might say more, but her husband wrapped his fingers around and under the waistband of her pants, using his hold to pull her back down to her seat, saying sternly, "That's enough, Lindsay. You'll scare her."

Over the school year, she fell so far for him that—although she wouldn't let him take even tastefully nude pictures of her—she even began to believe that he wasn't saying it insultingly or sarcastically when he complimented her or called her "little one" or "little girl". That was coming a huge way, for her!

And he did compliment her, all the time, and not just on her looks, but on the very advances he was helping her make. He noticed when he finally got her into the habit of just saying "thank you" when he praised her for something. And he cheered her on when she got brave enough to dance a slow dance with him, when they were alone at his place, with the fire lit and the lights down low. And he praised her especially, when she began to tell him of some of her more embarrassing experiences being overweight, and held her tight then kissed her tears away and gave her something to scream about instead.

She still got herself disciplined regularly, though. Even when summer rolled around again and they'd been together for nearly a year, she still got spanked pretty much as often as she had when they'd first gotten together—but for different reasons.

Of course, he'd had to announce the fact that this was their anniversary to everyone at the picnic while maintaining a death grip on her hand, even though she kept mumbling under her breath to him that it wasn't, really, technically.

Then he'd turned to her, and all it took now was a slightly raised-eyebrow look. He rarely even had to say her name anymore.

Jane could be a bit superstitious, and she knew that talking about such things was just tempting fate to come along and destroy them. And she had been terribly, terribly right.

She was staying at Eli's in order to be as much help with the shindig as possible. Lindsay and Jake were staying that night, too, since they would be there late, anyway, and everyone would have had booze. Jane had been helping with what seemed like the never ending clean up, but once they got all the food put away and the tables that had been set up for it cleaned and stowed away, they'd all gathered on the patio to listen to the music that they could hear people were already tuning up for.

She hadn't heard from Eli in longer than usual, although he was in demand at this thing. He ran it all—with help from his family and friends—and seemed to enjoy it, or he would have stopped doing it.

"Have you seen your long-lost brother?" she mentioned to Lindsay.

Lindsay frowned. "Come to think of it, no, I haven't. Not in a little while, anyway. He's usually buzzing in and out of the place. I wonder where he's gotten to?"

Jane put down the bowl she was drying and put her dish-towel into it. "If you don't mind, I'm going to see if I can find him."

Both Lindsay and Sheila, who was there, too, of course, turned to say in smarmy voices, "Of course not!"

"Can't be without him for more than a minute at a time, can you?" Sheila teased.

"Between the lines, the both of you," Jane returned, holding up her index, middle, and ring fingers together, then folding the two on the outside down to flip them both the bird.

She figured she should start in the house, and the most likely place to find him was the den—or his study, as he liked to call it. She thought that was a bit much, but whatever.

The door was closed, which was unusual, because he made a habit of keeping it open.

Not expecting that he was there, Jane gave a perfunctory knock and walked in.

The scene that greeted her eyes made her feel as if she'd been hit in the stomach with a sledge hammer.

Eli was there, all right, only he wasn't alone. Cindy Hart was with him. She was sitting on his big, sturdy desk—and she knew it was sturdy from her own personal experiences lying on it—with her legs spread wide around his thighs, skirt hiked up around her waist. His belt was already undone, and maybe his zipper was, too. Her mind didn't register that detail.

What it did register was that her mouth was open beneath his, her top down enough to reveal her breasts, and her slim arms were wrapped around Eli's neck.

And he didn't register one iota of protest until he saw Jane standing in the doorway with her hand over her mouth. He didn't push her away—hell, he should already have been pushing her away—he didn't make any excuses—he was stunned and frozen into a very compromising position.

She was gone almost before he saw her, and Eli saw his life pass before his eyes.

"Jane!" he yelled, fit to shake the rafters as he pulled the clinging woman's body off of his, then hurried after Jane, trying to rearrange his clothing as he ran.

She ran—well, she walked as quickly as she could—past the girls in the kitchen, tears streaming down her cheeks, her hand still over her mouth because she thought she was going to puke.

The girls left what they were doing and tore after her, finding her standing in the middle of the driveway that was kept clear for the family's vehicles, shoulders shaking as she cried.

"Jane, honey, what is it?" Sheila asked, coming to hug the shaking, sobbing woman.

She couldn't even get home! She didn't bring her car over here anymore, because they always went everywhere together!

"Jane!" Eli bellowed and kept bellowing, until Jake found him and they found the girls.

When he got there, she was bent over, she was crying so hard, and his sister and her friend were with her.

"Jane, I—it's not—it's not what you think it was," he said, but was that a lie? Had he been pushing Cindy away with all his might? Had he broken away from her hold—he certainly could have if he'd bothered. In his defense, he had started out trying to dissuade her gently, but he could hardly say any of that to Jane.

And it didn't help that Cindy had appeared, draping herself all over Eli, who kept slapping her hands away and moving away from her, which, he acknowledged baldly to himself, was what he should have been doing from the start.

Cindy was roaring drunk and it was only seven. "It was *exactly* what you think it was, Jane," she contradicted him. "He was way into me." Then she turned to press herself lewdly up against Eli. "You don't want to be with that fat pig, do you, when you could have this?"

Lindsay grabbed Cindy by the hair, which pried her off Eli when little else probably would have. "I think it's time to take out the trash."

Jake took over, putting the young woman, not particularly gently, into the passenger's side of his car. "I'll take her home. You both take Jane home and stay with her. Grab a bottle of booze. I think she'll need it."

Sheila took Jane's arm and helped her towards her car.

"Jane—" Eli said once, his hand out to her, but she wasn't

looking at him. She probably wouldn't look at him ever again.

Lindsay had brushed by him on the way in to get a bottle of something, and she didn't mince words when she walked by him on her way to Sheila's car. "Nice going, big brother. I would have thought better of you."

As the car took Jane away from him, for all intents and purposes permanently, he mumbled, "I would have thought better of me, too."

Lindsay and Sheila had spent the rest of the weekend at Jane's, keeping her phone away from her, keeping her off her computer and away from social media—like good friends do. And letting her get shit faced drunk—for the first time—for the first twelve hours or so, then holding her as she threw up —then helping her sober up and holding her as she wept pitifully.

Since it was summer vacation, Sheila didn't have anywhere to go Monday morning, but Lindsay did, so she said her goodbyes Sunday night and went back to her husband, telling Jane not to ever hesitate to get in touch with her if she needed anything.

Sheila figured she was going to be there for a while. But she was wrong. When she got up on Monday morning, Jane was already up.

"Did you sleep well?" Jane asked.

Sheila thought she was in the twilight zone. No signs of crying. Her eyes were completely clear. No rocking back and forth and moaning. She looked almost—but not quite —normal.

"Uh, yeah?"

"That's good. Do you want to go out for breakfast?"

"Uh, sure?"

"Good. You take your car, and I'll take mine, and then you can go home from Babe's."

It was their favorite breakfast place—cinnamon in the pancakes, doughnut muffins, and real maple syrup.

But when they ordered, Jane didn't get the usual short stack, eggs, hash browns, and sausage. Instead, she asked for two eggs scrambled, a grilled English muffin and turkey bacon.

Definitely in the twilight zone, Sheila concluded.

They had a pretty normal meal, which only added to her friend's suspicions, both avoiding that one particular subject, of course.

When they were done, Jane pushed her chair back.

"Wait. Are you sure you're going to be okay?" Sheila asked. "Because I'd be glad to stay with you."

Her friend gave her an almost eerily sane look. "You're sweet, but I'm fine."

"You're fine? You discovered the man that you've loved since I can remember—and who pretty much has presented himself as loving you right back—very nearly boffing the town skank, and you're fine, a couple days later?"

"Really. I am."

"You're not going to do anything stupid, are you?"

"Absolutely not."

"Good. Well, if you're sure you're okay, I'll go, but I'm gonna check in with you every five seconds."

"Go right ahead. I'll be home. I still have some work to do setting up my grade book for this year, then I'm going to start watching *Barry*. I've heard it's good."

All those months later, Eli and Jake were commiserating over a dinner that Eli had invited his brother-in-law to—without his lovely wife, which was probably better, since he'd largely been persona non-grata to her since he'd taken a flame thrower to what had been his very happy life.

This wasn't an unusual thing; the two men had gotten quite close since they'd met, about a year before Jake and Lindsay got married. They'd known of each other before-hand, crossed paths at meetings and other such dos, but they'd developed into quite tight friends.

Dinner—big, tender, juicy steaks, foot sized baked pota-toes, corn on the cob—all of it cooked on the grill, except dessert, which was the only one he knew how to make—brownies, but he intended to decorate them up by making them sundaes. They hadn't quite gotten to that point yet, but they were adjourning to the living room to watch some football.

With the both of them settled on the big couch, Jake got right to the point. "So, not that I don't appreciate your company and the hospitality, but why'd you invite me over here?"

Eli put the game on the big screen TV, but turned down the volume seconds later.

"Am I that transparent?"

"Yes, you are. And I heard that you drove Jane home from a bar last night."

The other man stiffened a bit, but he nodded as he took a pull from his beer. That was small town life for you. Everyone knew everyone else's business. "That I did. She was drunk. I'd never known her to take a drink, but she was really soused—almost fell down when she got up out of her chair, and I wasn't about to allow her to drive home."

Jake had frowned. "I haven't heard anything about her getting that way any other time, and you know that she and Lindsay are still close, so I'd hear about it if it was a habit."

"That's what I was hoping to hear."

"Why wouldn't you let her take the Uber, though?"

Eli fixed him with an accusatory glare. "And here I thought your standards were as high as mine. I wasn't about to let her get into a car—drunk—with a stranger, who was most likely a man."

Jake nodded. "Good point. And?"

The other man fidgeted, which he never did. "And I don't know. I just wanted a sympathetic ear."

"Bullpucky."

He frowned deeply. "Now I know why our women hate us."

"Mine doesn't, thank you very much." Jake raised his beer in salute.

Eli sighed. "Yeah, well, mine does, and, since I'm guilty as sin, I can't even begin to come up with a way to get her back. Why would she want me back? I ripped her heart out!"

"You didn't actually—" He'd never really asked, and Eli had never really volunteered any of the details.

"No, I didn't, but I wasn't fighting Cindy off very hard."

Jake cleared his throat. "Why don't you tell me the whole thing, and then maybe I'll be able to give you some advice, but I feel like I'm playing blind here, since I don't know what really happened in that room."

As much as he didn't want to, Eli went ahead and gave him all of the gory details.

And afterward, Jake took a long pull on his beer and said, "Well, son, you definitely fucked up."

Eli had to smile because Jake almost never swore, and he was always on Lindsay for doing so. Her potty-mouth probably accounted for the majority of her punishments, and he made a mental note to compliment Jake on his efforts later. She swore a lot less than she used to, and he'd noticed that when he was around her.

Which wasn't often lately because of what a bastard he was.

"Tell me something I don't know."

"Okay. You're beating yourself up too much. You didn't have sex with the woman."

"No, I didn't."

"If Jane hadn't come in, would you have screwed her?"

"Absolutely not!" Eli scoffed. "I was trying to get her off me, just not as forcefully as I think I should have."

"Do you want to have sex with Cindy Hart? You could right now, you know. You're free."

"Hell no! And it's not my being free that I worry about! Jane's free, now, too, and she could be with anyone!"

"I know." Jake took a breath. "I think you're raking yourself over the coals more than any man I know would for this. You feel guilty, and you should, to a certain extent. You can own that and practice self-flagellation for it as much as you want for as long as you want. But I think you should see Jane and tell her that you're incredibly sorry for what you did. Apologize to her deeply and sincerely, but point out to her that—as incriminating as things looked at the time—you didn't let it get very far. She knows what kind of woman Cindy is. Point out to her that, if you wanted her, you could have had her, long before this."

All of the points Jake was making made sense to him.

"But how am I going to get her to see me? She hates me."

Jake touched his arm. "Eli, you probably already know this, but you have a very devious sister, who would love nothing more than to play matchmaker and be able to say that she got you two back together."

He frowned. "What does Lindsay have to do with it?"

"You just leave it all up to me, my friend. We'll get things worked out for you."

Chapter 9

THAT FRIDAY, Sheila and Jane were going to have a girls' night at Lindsay's place. This was nothing new, and she didn't need to pack a bag or anything—Jane had stuff in a drawer in one of the guest rooms for just such a purpose.

When she arrived, she didn't see Sheila's car, but then, maybe she was late. Lateness from Sheila was not at all unexpected.

She didn't like to arrive empty handed, so she brought snacks, something wicked for the two of them—homemade, soft, chewy chocolate chip monster sized cookies, and something less sinful for herself—homemade granola.

"Oh, you brought food, thank you!" Lindsay had given her a perfunctory hug because she was already opening one of the plastic containers she'd relieved her of and was sinking her teeth into a cookie the size of her head and groaning orgasmically while doing so.

"Sheila's late, I take it?"

"Something like that, yes."

That should have tipped her off, but it didn't.

Jake appeared and hugged her more genuinely than her friend had.

"How are you?"

They'd become closer, too, while she was with Eli, and he had even continued to keep a weather eye out for her as best he could, operating as a bit of a pushy older brother, but Jane knew that he cared about her and she took it in the way it was intended.

"I'm fine, thanks!"

"No after affects from a week ago?"

"A week ago?"

"I think he's referring to when I brought you home because you'd had a bit too much to drink," Eli supplied, stepping out of the kitchen to face her.

He wasn't particularly close to her, but Jane still took two steps back, and Lindsay—and Jake—could see how much that hurt Eli.

But Jane couldn't. She was staring at the floor, arms crossed over herself.

Lindsay came forward to hug Jane, but she stepped away from that, too. "Look, I'm sorry we deceived you, but I really think you two should talk, maybe you could work things out. You're both so miserable without the other, we just wanted to see if we could help by bringing you together—on neutral territory—and then, maybe something good will come of it."

"We're going to leave you two alone," Jake added.

They ducked out of the house, and she was alone with him.

"You look amazing. You've always looked amazing, but you look healthier."

"Thinner?" she supplied pointedly.

Eli had never been so nervous in his life. "Well, yes, if you want to put it that way."

She didn't say anything else.

"Have you—have you been trying to lose weight?" he asked, scrambling for something to say to her and wishing he could get away from this volatile topic, but he couldn't seem to.

"Yes."

"Are you doing Weight Watchers, or what?"

She had been on her phone, but then she looked up at him and said in that horribly neutral tone he'd heard Friday night, too, "No, I stopped eating shit."

Eli chuckled. "Well, that'll do it."

He was surprised—and a little worried—that she was so unemotional. He expected crying and weeping and wailing, and she was just standing there. She'd done whatever on her phone, and now she was just looking at him with a blank expression on her face.

This wasn't going to work. He might as well say what he'd come here to say and let her go.

"Look, I'm sorry to get you here by tricking you, but I didn't figure you'd come if I asked you to talk to me at my place, and you wouldn't let me into your place—"

She didn't say a word, so he continued. "I wanted to tell you that..." Eli sighed long and loud, running his fingers through his hair. "...I screwed up. Cindy came onto me all of a sudden—her hands were everywhere—but I wasn't as fast or as definitive as I should have been in letting her know that I didn't want that. I wouldn't have let it go any further—I can't stand her! I've never been with her before, and I never will. I know I've caused you irreparable pain and suffering. It's my fault, and I just wanted to let you know how very, very sorry I am, and that I'll be sorry all of the rest of my days."

Stay focused! Don't respond! she kept telling herself. But it was very hard to accomplish, because this was Eli, and she was still in love with him. And that terrified her. And it kept her up at night. And it made her want to throw herself into his arms right now and feel them close around her as they had so many times before.

He took a few steps towards her, encouraged by the fact that she didn't move away from him. But her head was down now, and he wondered if she was crying.

"Did—did you call for an Uber?"

"Yes."

"I-I would be glad to take you home, if you'd like."

"That's not necessary, thank you."

Damn, she should have moved away from him, but he smelled so good, so familiar, and warm, and strong, and she couldn't deprive herself of the ability to be near him one last time, no matter how much it hurt her to do so.

And then he took another step closer, so that as she looked down, she could see his boots.

"Jane, honey."

Damn this man's voice! It wormed its way into her brain through her ear and began disassembling her defenses, brick by brick.

"Don't—don't call me that," she whispered urgently.

"All right, babygirl. Anything you say."

"Stop it, Eli!"

"Stop what, little girl?"

That was the one that got her. Jane raised her head, tears streaming down her cheeks, intending to give him what for, when his lips crashed down onto hers, and he lifted her into his arms, kissing and carrying her to the couch in Lindsay and Jake's living room at the same time.

At first, she refused to kiss him back, and he understood that.

But he was persistent, keeping her trapped in his arms on his lap until she began to soften and cry all the more because of it.

He'd wanted to hold her and comfort her for so long that

he closed his arms very tightly, before loosening them. "I'm sorry, did I hurt you?"

Jane shook her head. It had felt marvelous, like coming home, but she didn't say that.

Now, Eli was the one who was looking down. "Jane, I have no right to keep you here with me. I know that." His arms fell from around her, freeing her. "And I know I no longer have the right to ask anything of you, either."

He was being surprisingly conciliatory and docile.

At least, until his head came up and he caught her eyes, one hand cupping her cheek to hold her for another incredibly passionate kiss and the other claiming her back, forcing her to arch into him.

Then he backed off a bit. "But you know me, I think. I'm going to do both things, because…" His head bowed again, but then came right back up so he could look into her eyes. "Because I love you, Jane. I love you, and I think that what we had was something most couples never experience—a level of intimacy that I've never had before with any woman —and I don't want to throw that away. I want that with you again, little one."

Holy fuck, he loved her! She couldn't believe he had just said that!

"Are you asking me or telling me?"

"Yes."

That got a small smile out of her.

"My instincts want me to tell you, but I think I should ask you." He brought her chin up. "Do you think you could see your way to forgiving me enough to let me back into your life, Jane?"

Jane's breath hitched when she spoke. "I want to say yes, but I still hurt, Eli. A lot."

He enveloped her in his arms and hugged her to him. "I

know you do, babygirl. I know you do, and I'm so sorry for that. We'll take it slow, okay?"

She nodded. "I think I could agree to taking it slow, yes."

His elation made him feel absolutely high.

Then she said, "But no spankings."

"Do what now?" His face fell.

"No punishments."

"Whoa now, little lady, that's a terrible thought! You need firm guidance," he assured her, patting her bottom as he did so. "And you'd miss it if I didn't take you in hand when you needed it."

"I don't think so."

His lips found hers. "Then explain to me why you were always so much wetter after I'd tanned your hide, Janey?"

She knew she'd lost that argument with him—always would—but at least she was his Janey again!

Epilogue

IT WAS late at night and she'd had a bit too much to drink. That was by design of her boyfriend, who had plied her with excellent food he'd cooked himself and just a bit more liquor than she was used to.

He had abstained, himself, but he didn't think she had noticed that. He wanted all of his wits around him to witness this, if he managed to pull it off.

Eli was at his most charming self, and he had guided her carefully through the evening. He knew her easily well enough now that he didn't think he realized he was doing that, either, but then, he had worked very hard to earn her trust back after his terrible gaffe, and she knew—he hoped she knew—that she was absolutely safe with him.

The pool lights had been turned on, but not the patio lights.

Sated, in every way save one, he guided her out to the pool. Soft music was playing in the background, and he coaxed and cajoled her until she even danced with him a bit, making her laugh and encouraging her to take a sip of her drink every once in a while.

"I'm warm," he said, pulling his shirt away from his body. "Maybe all that time in the kitchen."

Jane snorted. "You were at the grill."

"Oh, well, still. I think I worked up a sweat. I'm going to take a swim."

Jane stood there, watching him, open mouthed, while he took off every stitch of clothing and jumped—bare assed naked—into the pool.

"Oh, that's it! That feels so good!" He was in the deep end, of course, which was quite deep, and treading water as he turned to her. "I haven't gotten you to swim with me yet! You owe me one! Come in, my love!"

He'd confessed his love to her, but she hadn't yet to him. He knew it was there—it was in everything she did for him, how she took care of him, how she obeyed him, and how she submitted herself to him when she didn't.

Eli had no doubt that she loved him—hell, she'd loved him a lot longer than he had her!

He did want to hear the words, but he didn't want to push her, so he'd never mentioned it. Eli was much too happy that he'd been granted a do over to push his luck.

"I don't have a suit," she mentioned softly.

"Neither do I, little love. It's just us. No agonizing bathing suits to try on or feel uncomfortable in while you're swimming. Just you and me and this deliciously refreshing water!"

She was standing, barefoot, at the edge of the pool, biting her lip and twisting her fingers, and he could have pulled her in, but he didn't want to do that.

He tried to be patient with her, but they both knew that he wouldn't wait forever. And if she couldn't get herself to where he wanted her to be, he wasn't above giving her the slightest push.

"Jane."

"But, Eli!"

"Tell me what makes you anxious about it, honey."

He hated it when she fretted when he didn't think she needed to, but he also recognized that was his judgment on the situation, not hers.

"I-I don't know."

"Nothing specific that you can name?"

"Nooo…"

She was such a good girl, always trying to behave for him.

"All right. How expensive are those clothes?"

Jane gave him a puzzled look and said, "Uh, they're from Goodwill. I think I paid seven dollars for the whole outfit. Why?"

"Well, then. Come in with your clothes on!"

He adored it when she smiled, and seconds later, he had her in his arms, wet clothes and all. But she wasn't wearing them for long, although she clung to each piece for some reason, needlessly, but he was firm.

"There—isn't that better?" he asked, when she was as naked as he was.

She had to admit that it was incredibly freeing! Jane swam a bit away from him and then back to where he was still near the side of the pool, and he took her in his arms again.

"I told you that you didn't need a bathing suit, Jane," Eli said, kissing her passionately. When he came up for air, he murmured, soft and low, "What you need so that you won't feel naked is a ring."

And with that, he put a very nice sized diamond ring on the third finger of her left hand.

"*Eli*! Jesus! Are you asking me—"

He was already shaking his head. "No way. I am *not* asking you to marry me. I am *telling* you that we're getting married, as soon as possible, my Janey."

She floated in his arms, but she could have done so without the water, considering how elated she felt.

"Even though you're a pushy bastard, I love you, Eli Ridgeway."

At that, he kissed her and dunked them both under the water.

The End

Carolyn Faulkner

The words "spanking" and "discipline" have always sent a shiver up Carolyn Faulkner's spine. She knows she's not alone. Writing started as a way to explore her feelings. Soon short stories flowed from her pen featuring reluctant heroes taking the leading lady in hand, but always for her own good.

Today Carolyn is the author of dozens of books. She writes from her home in Maine, where she lives with her husband and leading man.

You can read an interview with Carolyn here:
http://www.blushingbooks.com/blog/?p=175

You may check out her website while it's under construction here:
http://www.carolynfaulkner.com

Don't miss these exciting titles by Carolyn Faulkner and Blushing Books!

Series books
Military Daddies
Lieutenant Daddy
Captain Daddy
Colonel Daddy
Major Daddy

Gentle Series

Her Gentle Giant
Her Gentle Cowboy
Her Gentle Soldier
Her Gentle Gangster
My Book
The Alpha's Woman series
The Alpha's Woman
Kosh's Omega
Red's Mate
An Omega's Awakening
The Omega Within
Mate of the Omega Collection

Adored series
Adored
Tessa's Wedding

The Red Petticoat Saloon series
Grading Garnet

Thornton Brothers trilogy
AJ's Hope
Beau's Desire
Cade's Wish
Thornton Brothers, Three-Book Set

Taken as His series
Prima
Tria

Priceless Love series
Priceless
Love's Possession
Dangerous Love

The Lark and The Bull
Doctor's Orders
A Babygirl for Christmas
Her Handyman
The Hart of the Matter
At His Hand
King of Hearts
True Desires
Lord Belden's Baggage
In His Care
Correct Me If I'm Wrong
Beauty Of The Beast
Tamed To His Hand
Daddy!
Amanda and the Stable Master
Lion
The Banished King
Northern Belle
The Cherished One
Forever Wife
Grace's Demon
Beauty's Beast
Captured by the Count
Male Order Bride
Sinful
Packed: The Enforcer
Submissive Love
A Heart Full of Heaven
Daddy's Girl
To Love a Man
Etta's Surrender
Her Secret Submission
Make Me
Let Me In

Tears of a Vampire, and Vlad's Story, Two-Book Set
Never Say Never
Under the Cover of Love
Her Guardian Don
Her Knight In Faded Denim
Forever In Love
Depths of Desire
The Power Of Love
Only Her
On the Razor's Edge of Paradise
Indiscreet
A Most Unsuitable Mate
Make Me Yours
Ready For Love
The Gentleman Dom
The Supplicant
Belonging
Hidden Desires
Her Bad Boy
All Is Right With the World
The Error Of Her Ways
<u>At His Hand</u>

Holiday Stories
A Holiday to Remember
Griff's Christmas Angel
<u>A Season to Submit</u>

Anthologies
Tamed By The Cowboy
Blushing Cheeks Vol. 1
12 Naughty Days of Christmas2017
12 Naughty Days of Christmas 2021
Dominating His Valentine

Blushing Books

Blushing Books is one of the oldest eBook publishers on the web. We've been running websites that publish spanking and BDSM related romance and erotica since 1999, and we have been selling eBooks since 2003. We hope you'll check out our hundreds of offerings at http://www.blushingbooks.com.

Blushing Books Newsletter

Please join the Blushing Books newsletter
to receive updates & special promotional offers.
You can also join by using your mobile phone:
Just text **BLUSHING** to 22828.